Bright

— A NOVEL —

CHRISTINE MELCHIOR

ISBN: 978-0-578-86383-2

DEDICATION

To my beautiful mother, Evelyn Leamy,
who believed there was nothing I could not do.

ACKNOWLEDGMENTS
WITH GRATITUDE

Bright would not have been completed without the love and support of the following people:

My awesome and dear husband Don, who has enthusiastically championed my writing and all my endeavors, and didn't let me give up when I hit those bumps in the road.

My exceptional and talented readers, Mary Ann Egan, Joann Sallmann, and Deborah Telles, whose generosity with time, wise feedback and deep friendship made *Bright* a better novel.

A special group of amazing women, my former colleagues, Jayne Mattson, Trisha Griffin Carty, Sallyann Kakas, Marilyn Morgan, and Louisa Mattson, who have continuously showered me with encouragement, and cheered me on for a very long time.

My writing friends, Susan Chernilo, Sue Hand, and Mary Wasmuth, who participated with me in writing groups, conferences and hours spent in the Weston Library. They kept me motivated and excited as we learned the craft together.

My long-time friend, Ann Sapira, whose compassion and extensive background in psychology and human behavior have provided me insights, which I've applied to my writing and my life.

Deepest gratitude goes to Joanne Parsons, long-time friend, author, editor, and writer-extraordinaire and the most gifted teacher I've had since beginning writing years ago. In the middle of crafting her third work of fiction, she took time to care about my novel. She read and critiqued it more times than she probably wants to remember. Her awesome imagination, instincts, humor, and talent have made me a better writer.

BRIGHT

CHAPTER 1

WESTERN MASSACHUSETTS, Town of Berkshire Ridge
March, 1983

Explosions rumbled the earth beneath her feet. Flames stretched toward the night sky, tinting it orange. There were no stars visible, no bright March moon. Sirens in the distance announced fire engines from neighboring towns racing toward the Mechanics Garage. Leeann Bright pictured cars and trucks melting into pools of plastic and metal. The smell of chemicals and gasoline drifted across the street and toward the parking lot of Loden's Family Tavern, where she stood outside her father's truck, and it made her gag. Her father was in the driver's seat lighting a cigarette. She climbed in.

"Tell me how the fire started." She wrapped her arms around herself.

"Don't ask," he snapped, pulling onto the two-lane road to home.

"What were you doing at the Garage, Dad? What happened?"

"Stop asking questions," he said, avoiding Leeann's eyes. He pressed on the brakes and slowed down. "Listen Leeann, you can never tell anyone you saw me running from the Garage."

"I can tell Mom, can't I?"

Her father rolled the truck to a stop. "The fire *was* an accident, but it may not look like an accident," he said. "With my luck, the police would finger me with arson. You want me to get convicted for something I didn't do? You want me to go to prison?" She shook her head, thinking what child would not cover up to protect a parent? In Berkshire Ridge, at the base of the Berkshire Mountains, where everybody knew everybody else's business, people didn't go to prison. There was no student at Fogg Middle School who had a parent serving time. She wouldn't be the first.

"You tell no one. Promise?"

Leeann gulped. "Promise." But she knew she wasn't good at keeping secrets, and she had a good excuse—she was twelve years old. When excitement got the best of her, before she knew it, the secret was out, floating in the air for all to hear. Her father knew that too. Maybe that's why he wrinkled his brow and gunned the gas. He swerved around a corner, leaving the pavement and bouncing on gravel and mud before gaining control. Leeann put her hands over her eyes. "Dad, you almost decimated that man's mailbox." Her voice trailed to a whisper.

Ninety minutes earlier
Leeann and her father, Richard Bright, were finishing a meal of codfish and coleslaw at Loden's. Richard downed a couple

shots of scotch. Twice, he pushed back his sleeve and checked his watch. After dinner, they made their way to the tavern's poolroom. Leeann jabbed billiard balls with a cue stick, sending them careening across the green felt surface of the pool table. She paused for her father's instruction.

"Decide where you want the cue ball to go after it sends your object ball into the pocket," her father said. He swallowed the last of his third scotch and glanced out the window. A yellow swizzle stick dangled from his mouth.

Leeann walked around the table, tilted her head sideways, her red hair grazing the table's edge, and gauged her line of aim. Her hips and legs remained so still she thought she could feel the blood moving through her veins. Resolve spread down her arms and into the fingers gripping the cue stick, as she placed it on the mount she formed with her outstretched left hand.

"Easy," her father urged. His bushy red hair draped the back of his neck.

Leeann jabbed her stick forward, sending the cue ball into the red ball head on. It rolled and dropped into a corner pocket. Her father nodded. The eyes of two men, the Hannah brothers, were on her too, and Leeann soaked up their attention. She walked to the opposite side of the table. A second setup and easy stroke sent the final ball, a solid yellow, into the pocket. Leeann threw her arms in the air.

She 'high-fived' her father's out-stretched hand.

"You're better than I was at your age."

Leeann liked having him all to herself on nights like this when her mother went to quilting class in the basement of St.

Mary's Church. She wanted to continue shooting pool, but the Hannah brothers wedged themselves between her and the pool table and began racking up the balls.

Her father pushed back his sleeve and looked at his watch again. "I need to see someone in the other room," he told her. "Stay right here until I come back. Watch the Hannah brothers play and learn something." The Hannahs were twins, about Leeann's father's age, and worked construction in town. One was tall with a large forehead and black curly hair, the other, much shorter and bald. Neither was friendly with anyone other than each other. Tonight, Leeann didn't want to watch the Hannahs play pool. Although she'd seen them at Loden's many times, she didn't know their first names. It seemed everyone in town referred to them as the Hannah Brothers or the Hannahs, nothing else. The short, bald brother knocked a bottle onto the floor, and beer splashed all over Leeann's new sneakers. She narrowed her eyes and squeezed her lips tight, squelching the words that formed in her head: *Hey, knucklehead, you're drenching me in beer.* She made a dramatic display of wiping her sneakers with big strokes of her hand and looking at the brothers every so often. They didn't seem to notice.

Tired of pool and the Hannah brothers, Leeann cruised around the crowded dining room. Patrons sat at tables covered with green tablecloths topped with white candles and vases of wilted flowers. She walked past a white balloon anchored to an empty table and gave it a punch.

Leeann pushed her way through the cramped sports lounge where loud music competed with noisy sports fans cheering the televised Bruins game. She wove through a sea of towering bodies, mostly men out of work since Williams Dye Works closed its doors a month before. A waitress maneuvering a tray of food knocked Leeann into the back of a tall man. He towered over her, and his scratchy plaid shirt smelled like a dead animal. Leeann moved away, uttering an apology, even though the collision wasn't her fault.

A sad-eyed, dusty, mounted rainbow trout hung on the wall over the bartender's head. Its marble eyes looked as if they were staring into Leeann's. She often stopped and stared back. Tonight, she didn't care about a stuffed fish. Her father wasn't at the bar either.

"Are you lost?" Bartender Will asked.

"Not me, my dad." Leeann headed back to the poolroom and the Hannah brothers to wait until her father showed up. She walked down the hallway toward the restrooms and a door used for deliveries. Catching a glimpse of her father hurrying out the door, she followed.

Richard Bright crossed the parking lot, still damp from the day's rain. He raced diagonally across the road and ducked into the woods. Leeann crossed the street and entered the woods, too. A hundred feet in, trees cleared, leaving a view of Mechanics Garage. Leeann knelt on a mat of wet leaves and waited. Dampness seeped into her jeans at the knees, through the denim patches her mother had ironed on that morning. A stump that looked like a gravestone jutted from the ground. Leeann grabbed it to steady herself. The only light at the foot of the incline ahead was the blinking of a neon sign in the window of the Berkshire Ridge Mechanics

Garage. It was where her father worked, but he wouldn't be going to work at this hour.

Leeann shivered as she crouched in the shrubs. She looked around at the blackness of the night, afraid if she took a step in the wrong direction, she'd drop off the edge of the world, or like Alice in Wonderland, tumble into a rabbit hole. A rustling noise broke the stillness. Her courage shriveled as she envisioned an animal crouching—a raccoon or fox. Her breathing became rapid. She thought about running back to the tavern, to the poolroom and the Hannah brothers, but her legs wouldn't move. Her eyes locked on the direction of the noise behind her until she was sure no danger lurked. When she faced forward again, smoke was rising from Mechanics Garage. Leeann dug her fingers into the rotted stump and watched flames erupt from the building. Backlit from the fire, Leeann's dad raced up the hilly path away from the blaze. She ran toward him, reaching out.

"What the hell are you doing here?" He didn't wait for an answer. They sprinted the short distance through the woods, across the road and back to the parking lot of the tavern. The wind blew dirt from the ground and spewed it against their shoes and pants. The security light in the parking lot illuminated her father's red flannel shirt and wild eyes.

He grabbed Leeann by the shoulders. "I told you to stay by the pool table."

"I saw you go out the back door."

"I went out to the truck to get your jacket. That's what you saw and that's what you say if anyone asks. We were never in the woods. I was never at the Garage. You saw nothing. Do you understand?" His chest heaved.

Leeann lowered her head.

Richard Bright grabbed his daughter's brown jacket from the truck. "Put it on." He threw the jacket at her. "Look at me, you saw nothing," her father whispered through gritted teeth. "Never speak to anyone about what happened over there."

"I didn't see anything."

"That's right. You saw me go out to the truck to get your jacket. After a minute, you followed me out. We sat in the truck while I finished a cigarette. We were outside no more than five minutes." Leeann nodded.

"It was an accident," he mumbled. He pushed Leeann inside, toward the jukebox. A Bob Dylan song, Mr. Tambourine Man, filled the dining room.

An instant of silence fell over Loden's after the first explosion, then excitement. A woman sitting near the front door jumped up and pointed to the window. "Fire." A waitress dialed 911. Patrons spilled onto the front lawn. Some stood in the middle of the country road as Ladder Nine passed them and swerved onto the rutted dirt road leading to the Garage. Leeann, her father, and a larger crowd walked into the woods and watched the fire from the end of the tree line where moments before Leeann had been kneeling. The fire lit the sky, providing a clear view of the scene and firefighters running in all directions, carrying hoses and hollering orders to one another. Leeann stood apart from the crowd on a half-crumbled stonewall. Smoke rolled over the treetops, and flames shot out of every window. Leeann couldn't turn her head away. Her face grew hot as the heat intensified. She tasted particles of soot. Others waved their hands in front of their faces in search of clean air.

"Damn shame you're out of a job tomorrow, Rich," one Hannah brother said.

"And a lot of other guys," her father answered, not taking his eyes off the blaze. "This is too much for my daughter. I'm taking her home."

CHAPTER 2

EASTERN MASSACHUSETTS, Boston and surrounding suburbs
1998

"You're breaking up Traci, speak louder." Leeann got up from her desk as though standing could help her better absorb Traci's remarks. She pressed the phone against her ear and plugged her other ear with one finger.

"I said it's reckoning time for someone."

"Where are you?" Leeann asked.

"Standing on a beam at the ledge of the thirty-third floor of a high-rise under construction." Traci was crew supervisor for Dressano Construction in Boston, the first female supervisor hired by the company in its fifty-year history.

Leeann stumbled over her briefcase on the carpeted floor. She too, worked in a Boston high-rise. From her office window, through squares of tinted glass, she took in a view of the city skyline, the airport, and the Atlantic Ocean. The sun poured light across her Chinese lacquered cherry wood credenza in a corner. She realized the high-pitched hum that filled her ears was not static but the sound of wind circling the construction site. She slapped her hand against her chest. "Get away from that ledge, Traci," she said to her friend. "You *are* wearing a safety harness, yes?"

"Of course."

"Traci, what are you trying to tell me?"

"Seems there's a break in the Mechanics Garage case."

"Fifteen years later?"

"Damning evidence has surfaced."

Leeann's heart pounded. Her breathing became shallow.

"I have to cut this short. The boss is flailing his arms at me," Traci said. "Some sort of emergency."

"Wait, tell me about the evidence."

"Come to my house tomorrow."

It was the second Saturday in March. Leeann Bright left her house in Concord mid-morning, braving a rain-driven Nor'easter, and headed for Traci Stylofski's house. Hailstones banged on her windshield. She drove along the familiar route, lined with bare maple trees, north to Medina where Traci and her husband Jimmy lived in a custom-designed colonial on two acres of land.

Thoughts raced through her mind. What evidence might have surfaced? Fibers? DNA? A confession? Did a witness come forward after years of silence? Leeann considered, for the first time, the possibility that her father had met someone at Mechanics Garage on the night of the fire. She'd heard stories of people coming forward years after they'd witnessed a traumatic event. It did happen.

She wondered where this so-called evidence might lead. If the truth came out that she lied for years to protect her father, she'd be charged with a crime. Worse, the news of the lie would kill Traci. Leeann tried to clear her mind and turned on the radio.

The rain came down harder, clouding trees and dead grass along her route. She passed apple orchards and open fields separating clusters of center-enter colonials. On one side of the road was the rain-swollen Bear River, the same color gray as the sky that afternoon. After a left at a fork, she pulled into Traci's winding driveway. Ahead of her was the house, bright red, audacious, like a Mid-western cow barn. That was Jimmy for you, loud and audacious—he'd chosen the color. Leeann liked him. His was the laugh you heard over the buzzing of voices in a restaurant. He was the one who verbalized what no one else would. An IT professional, he drove a motorcycle to work. He stood out in a crowd with his big personality. And Traci adored him.

The interplay of evergreens and leafless ornamental trees in front of their house held Leeann's attention until Traci opened the front door and waved. Leeann thought her friend still looked like the twelve-year-old girl she befriended after the fire. She could almost see those freckles and long neck. As a kid, Traci cut her own hair, aiming for a Dorothy Hamill wedge. The Olympic ice skater was her idol. The result was a heavy metal rocker-girl look, short and spikey and a little jagged in the back. Not too different from her hair today, although now styled by a professional.

Leeann remembered their bike rides to Mel's Café for ice cream after school. She never wavered from her favorite, a large vanilla cone, and ordered Traci a double scoop, one strawberry, the other chocolate chip.

As kids, Traci rode in Leeann's shadow. Nowadays, it was Leeann who stood in awe of her friend. Traci put herself through four years of Boston Engineering College while working three jobs. A successful career and marriage seemed to come easy to her. She knew how to fix a furnace, assemble a lawnmower, and drive an eighteen-wheeler. And she wouldn't say a bad word about anyone if her life depended on it.

Traci hopped down her front stairs, a golf umbrella in her hands. "Run," she called out.

Leeann raced from her car to the porch, jumping over puddles and clasping her rain-soaked hood under her chin. Her purse flapped in the wind.

"Tell me about this damning new evidence," Leeann said. She wiped water from her face.

"Can we at least get inside the house?"

A bottle of Chilean Sauvignon Blanc, a bowl of hummus, and French bread awaited them in the den. Traci poured them each a glass.

"So what's going on?" Leeann asked again.

Traci grabbed the remote control and turned on the Bruins game. She muted the volume. "You remember that Josh Wilson works for *The Advocate*, right?"

"I remember he had leukemia, too. Once as a kid and again a year ago."

"Yeah, and he beat it. Since then, he's been editor of the paper."

"He was always a go-getter," Leeann added.

"He's writing an article on the fifteenth anniversary of Mechanics Garage fire."

Leeann let out a groan. "Why?"

"Why not? People in town remember it. The arsonist was never caught. He or they are out there somewhere. Josh wants to interview me because my dad died there, as you well know."

"What about the new evidence?"

"Oh yeah, the evidence." Traci brushed bangs from her eyes.

"An anonymous note was sent to Josh at the paper," Traci said. She threw her feet onto the coffee table. "It implicates someone. He wouldn't say who, but he wants my advice figuring out what to do next."

"*Your* advice? Did he go to the police?"

"No, could be a hoax. The paper always gets crap from disgruntled people."

"Hardly sounds like damning evidence, Traci." Leeann relaxed her shoulders and sat back on the sofa.

"Josh said it could be nothing or it could be very damning."

"I'll bet it implicates Roland Barnes. He was one mean bastard. His employees couldn't stand him."

Leeann turned her eyes to the TV, and Traci turned up the volume. Over the next hour, they argued over what Leeann thought were some pretty bad calls from the referees. When the game was over, she stretched her arms over her head, and a little bone cracked in her shoulder.

"Did you hear that? I need to work out more." She stood up and on a nearby desk spotted a silver-framed photo of Traci and Jimmy and Ben and her, taken the year before skiing in Vermont. She wished she hadn't seen it.

"You look glum."

"The photo."

"Leeann, I'm sorry. I should have put it away."

"I've been in a bad mood since Ben and Gentle Giant Movers cleared his things out of my house a week before Thanksgiving, a hundred seventeen days ago."

Traci folded her arms across her chest. She looked as if she was forming some sympathetic thought in her mind and was about to deliver it. Instead, she said, "Let me show you the porch Jimmy and I are building. You can hammer nails to vent your fury at Ben."

Leeann raved about the job Traci and Jimmy did building the porch. They'd done a lot of the work in winter, Traci said, when temperatures hovered around freezing. She showed Leeann how they stretched the screen over the wooden frame, where they placed the nails, and what size nails they used. "Here try banging a few."

With her left hand, Leeann held a nail against a section of wood, and with her right hand, she swung. She missed the nail, hammered her thumb, and blood oozed around her fingernail. Pain shot up her arm and she let out a string of obscenities.

"Let's fix up your hand," Traci announced. "Don't quit your day job. You'll never make it in construction."

They returned to the den where Traci handed Leeann another glass of wine. She stammered, "I told Josh he could interview you, too."

"Why'd you tell him *that*?" Leeann pinched her eyes closed as if in pain.

"Because I don't want to go to Berkshire Ridge alone."

"The place depresses me. Go with Jimmy," Leeann said, wiping her hands on her jeans.

"He won't go with me," Traci said, biting her lip, an old habit from childhood. "He's living with his sister. Jimmy and I separated."

Leeann raised her eyebrows.

"We've got issues. Don't want to talk about it."

"You're the last two people…why?"

"Drop it, please. Right now I'm asking you to come with me to the interview."

Leeann held up her bandaged thumb. "Can't go, I'm incapacitated." She headed to the bathroom. A few minutes later, she found Traci loading the dishwasher. Leeann studied the drooping orchid sitting on the sill. "It's a miltonia orchid."

"Jimmy bought it a couple weeks ago. Looked nice until he left."

Jimmy was the gardener in the family, and Leeann figured the drooping orchid didn't have a snowball's chance in hell with Traci taking care of it. Traci would have agreed. She couldn't nurture a green thumb no matter how hard she tried, no matter how much instruction Leeann had given her over the years. Traci gave the orchid a spot check. "I may be turning all my plants over to you." She lifted her head, and standing in front of Leeann, begged her again to go with her to Berkshire Ridge. "Come on, you've got nothing better to do."

"Ouch, that hurt. I do have a highly demanding career."

"You work too much."

Leeann ignored the comment. They returned to the living room and Leeann glanced in a mirror above Traci's fireplace. Traci took a seat on the sofa and kicked off her shoes.

"You sure you don't want to talk about Jimmy?" Leeann asked.

Traci shook her head.

"Okay then, let me ask you a question. Why do you think Ben refused to make a commitment to me?"

"Forget him. You're a catch. You're skinny, fit, and gorgeous."

"No seriously. I know I have a prominent chin and fat ankles. And my elbows are ugly with the psoriasis I get fairly often. But Ben always said I looked good. And we had a great relationship."

"There's nothing wrong with you."

"No, dig deep. What's one thing that could have bothered him about me?"

"Well, let me think." Traci lifted her head to the ceiling and squinted. "You can be guarded at times. You know, closed off."

"What?"

"You don't self-disclose. You hold back when people try to get to know you."

Leeann flushed scarlet. "Now you're a shrink? Guarded? Me?"

Traci poured herself another glass of wine. "You're smart, funny, lovable, but yes, guarded."

"You're insane. No one's ever called me guarded. Drop the subject."

"Fine, I'm just sayin'."

CHAPTER 3

WESTERN MASSACHUSETTS, Berkshire Ridge
March, 1983
Leeann Bright, 12 years old

L eeann woke the day after the fire, hoping no one would mention it again. She went to the kitchen and poured a bowl of Frosted Flakes.

Her mother was making coffee. "Last night's fire was a horrible tragedy."

Leeann swallowed a spoonful of cereal. "Mom, can we not talk about it?"

Her mother stood behind her and grasped her daughter's shoulders. "A man died in the fire. It was Traci Stylofski's father, Norm."

Leeann felt a shiver run through her. Traci sat next to her at school. Her father was a janitor and locksmith until his drinking made him incapable of holding down either job. It was common knowledge in town that Norm was known to break into businesses with a bottle of liquor and pass out for the night.

Her father entered the kitchen and reached for a mug of coffee.

"Did you hear the news, Rich, that Norm Stylofski was killed in the fire last night?" She sat down at the table. "It's all over the TV."

Richard Bright slammed his mug into the sink. The cup broke into pieces, sending coffee across the counter and onto the white café curtain. He sat hard onto a kitchen chair. The color drained from his face. Leeann glanced at him. She ran to her room, grabbed her backpack, and left for school. Traci was absent from class.

Police began interviewing everyone who'd been inside Loden's on Tuesday night. On Thursday, two days after the fire, a detective was coming to the house to interview Leeann. Over breakfast, and while his wife slept, Leeann's father told her how important it was to answer questions as he instructed her. After school again, in the truck, idling in front of the family's green-shuttered cape, he helped Leeann practice fielding questions.

Richard Bright was known to greet people with wariness, but today he was jovial in his welcoming of Detective John Handley, new to the town's police force. Leeann stood back, assessing Detective Handley. She thought he was much older than her father and fantasized trimming the mustache hanging over his top lip.

Helene Bright, usually gracious and outgoing, was standoffish and brusque. "I don't like the idea of my daughter being interrogated."

"This isn't an interrogation, Mrs. Bright. We're gathering statements from everyone who was at the tavern the night of the fire."

Leeann's father removed a package of light bulbs and a portable radio from one of the chairs, and they each took a seat at the kitchen table. Leeann, at the head, rubbed her hands together. Her eyes darted around the room as the officer pulled a flimsy notebook from his pocket and searched for a blank page. Her father sat opposite her on the edge of his chair. He lit a cigarette. Helene Bright took the seat next to her daughter, her hands wrapped around a cup of hot tea.

Handley put down his notebook and leaned close to Leeann. His glasses sat halfway down his nose. "Don't look so scared, Leeann, you've done nothing wrong. I've got a couple questions that won't take up much of your time." Leeann nodded. Handley looked at the pink plastic clock on the far wall as if he, like the family, wanted to get this meeting over with.

The skinny man in a baggy suit asked his first question. "What were you doing at Loden's on Tuesday night?"

"Had dinner with my dad. Played pool. Watched the Hannah brothers play pool."

"Did you talk to anyone other than your dad?"

Leeann scratched her head. "Patty the waitress. Will the bartender."

Handley scribbled in his notebook. "Did you see anyone acting strange or hostile or disruptive? Anybody getting into any fights?" He posed the question without any real interest as if he'd asked it hundreds of times before.

Leeann hadn't anticipated this question. She stared at her mother's teacup and her fingers, which were not slim and dainty and ivory-smooth, but thick and stubby with short nails from working the soil at the nursery she owned in town. She had calluses on the tips of her fingers and dryness over the tops of her knuckles. "The Hannahs were kinda drunk. They were fighting with each other."

Her father nodded.

Handley scribbled some more. "Did anyone leave by the back door?"

"I saw my dad go out to get my jacket."

"How long was he gone?"

Leeann's eyes rested on the kitchen table's yellow Formica top. The sun moved behind the clouds as the room, once bright, grew dark.

"A minute or so," she replied.

"And then?"

The words she'd practiced with her father echoed in her head. "Then I went out to get him."

"Where was he?"

"In the truck having a cigarette. We sat in the truck for five minutes while he finished the cigarette, then we went back inside with my jacket. Then we heard a woman yell that there was a fire across the street. That's it." She shrugged.

"And you saw no one hanging around the doors or the parking lot?"

Leeann tugged at her chin. Her eyes roamed the room. "I'm thinking of something."

"Go ahead, say it," her mother urged.

"Don't push her, Helene," Leeann's father said.

"Do you remember something?"

Leeann looked at her father. "I can't…"

"Say it, sweetie," her mother continued. "You can't what?"

"No one else left or entered," Leeann said with conviction. "That's right, I remember now, yes." She looked to her father for a signal that she was doing a good job but all she saw was a blank expression. Within that blank face, Leeann saw Traci's father lying on the ground, the room filling with smoke around him. She closed her eyes and shook her head.

"You're shaking your head, Leeann," Handley said. "As if you're saying one thing but thinking something else. You've got to be truthful with me, right?"

"Don't go after my daughter like that," her father shouted.

"Richard, please." Helene waved her hand.

Handley paused to adjust the glasses that had slipped further down his nose, which, like his entire face, was damp with sweat. "Did you ask your dad to get your jacket or did he get it without your asking?"

This was another question Leeann hadn't anticipated, and her heart raced. She tried to calm herself by taking deep breaths and staring at the linoleum beneath her feet. Her eyes moved to the wall, to the tiles above the kitchen sink. Some were cracked, others missing, leaving a brown, dried-up, gummy surface in plain view.

"Take your time and think," her mother offered.

"Do you remember, Dad?" Leeann asked. She let out a loud exhale.

"I went to the truck without your asking." He propped his elbows onto the table. A cigarette dangled from his fingertips.

"That's right, I remember." Leeann couldn't wait to get the detective out of the house.

"Anybody seem obsessed with watching the fire?"

"Now really, how would my daughter know that?" Leeann's father stood up, signaling the interview was over.

Her mother stood up, too. "I don't see how this was any help to you but I guess you have a job to do." She ran her hand through her thick, dark hair.

Handley, apparently, had enough, too. He offered Leeann his hand, which she shook tentatively.

"Leeann remembers the events as I described them to you," her father said.

"Yes, the statements are identical," Handley answered, giving Leeann's father a sideways stare and shoving his notebook into his pocket.

Leeann's father opened his mouth as if he were about to protest.

"I meant everyone's story is consistent. No one's reported anything out of the ordinary." Handley walked to the front door, stepping around a knee-high stack of yellowed newspapers and a case of soda. He thanked the family for their time.

Leeann swung her arms by her side. She hadn't made one mistake. She knew she'd done a good job because her father put his hands on her shoulders. Standing at the sink, rinsing her cup, Leeann's mother shook her head and muttered, "That was a waste of everyone's time."

That night Leeann's mother stuck her head in to her daughter's room. "Time for bed." Leeann climbed under the sheets. "We're all sad about the fire and Dad losing his job," she said. "Try to put all this out of your mind."

"I will, Mom."

Her mother turned off the light and closed the door.

Leeann clutched her pillow to her stomach. The fire wouldn't leave her alone. She cried for Traci and Norm Stylofski. When she drifted off, she saw her father outrunning an orange fireball through the woods. During hours of fitful sleep, she tried to imagine how the fire started. She settled on believing her father dropped a cigarette in the dried brush in front of the garage. She tossed from side to side. It killed her to have to keep the secret from her mother. She'd always told her everything with the exception of the time she smoked a cigarette with Josh Wilson behind the middle school. And, of course, she never told her mother about the times she waded in Misty Creek. Her mother had warned her to stay away from it. She'd said it spawned horrible, disease-causing bacteria but couldn't come up with the names of any grotesque diseases they caused. She tried not to disobey her parents, dreading the punishment from her father, especially. Her mother's punishment banned her from television for a day. But her father issued sarcastic reprimands and withdrew his attention for days after the offense. He was capable of fits of rage but reserved them mostly for Leeann's mother.

Leeann woke in the middle of the night on a sweat-soaked sheet. Panic tightened her chest. She sat up, trying to catch her breath. She had lied to the police and that was a crime. She broke the law. People get arrested for lying to the police. They get prosecuted. She could end up in jail or juvenile hall for a long time. She took deep breaths trying to relax and clear her mind. Her eye caught a patch of blue and yellow paisley patterned wallpaper, dimly lit by her night-light. When she squinted, she saw sea urchins with monster heads floating across the wall.

CHAPTER 4

WESTERN MASSACHUSETTS, Berkshire Ridge
March, 1983
Leeann Bright, 12 years old

The funeral mass for Norm Stylofski took place at St. Mary's Church on Saturday. Mourners braved the aftermath of the snow that fell the night before, burying Berkshire Ridge in layers of icy powder and transforming cars into rows of round white haystacks. Leeann raced through the unplowed parking lot to get to the church doors, skidded on a patch of ice, but managed to stay upright. Her mother, holding onto to her husband's arm, scolded her for not being careful.

The Bright family sat in the third row and watched Traci break down as she followed her father's casket. Mr. Stylofski's three older daughters walked together covering their faces. His wife walked alone clutching rosary beads to her lips.

Leeann and her mother huddled shoulder to shoulder, shivering in the cold church. Hymns droned from the organ in the balcony. Leeann struggled to pay attention during the mass. The priest spoke too long, and her thoughts drifted to upcoming summer days. The smoky scent of incense brought her back to the present.

Leeann, her parents, and a line of mourners followed Traci's family to the church cemetery. Leeann thought the priest's feet must be as numb as hers because she heard his teeth chattering. He was quick with the prayers at the gravesite.

Leeann's mother and father held her hand as they made their way back on deep snow to their car. A man approached Leeann's parents and introduced himself as Norm's brother Ray from Boston. Bundled in a fur coat and wearing a gold stud in his ear lobe, he looked out of place among the residents of Berkshire Ridge.

"I refused to speak to Norm for years. Stupid family argument over money," Ray said. Wisps of his hair waved in all directions with each gust of wind. Ray hurried to keep pace with Leeann's parents as they marched, heads down, through the snow. "People are saying my brother set that fire."

Leeann's mother answered. "No one believes that."

"Norm Stylofski never hurt anybody," Ray insisted.

Leeann's father turned around and walking backwards said, "If it was Norm, he didn't do it maliciously. Dropped a match, maybe."

"Ya got gasoline and oil and toxic fumes everywhere in the garage. That fire started on its own," Loden's bartender Will added, following closely behind Leeann's father. "You worked there, Rich. Wasn't it a tinder box waiting for a spark?"

Richard Bright shrugged. "Could have been electrical. Roland didn't keep his garage up to code."

"You're missing the obvious," Leeann's mother said. "There could be an arsonist living among us. People are asking, 'Is my business next?' "

Will shivered, standing at the edge of the church graveyard. "Fire Marshall's findings should be out any day."

"Ray," Leeann's mother began, "Norm's family is right behind us. Why don't you join them?"

"No."

"Go ahead, it could be a new start."

"I tried yesterday. They walked away from me."

No one said a word. All Leeann heard was the sound of boots breaking through crusty snow. A deer jumped out of a clump of trees, and all eyes followed it across the lawn until it disappeared over a hill. When Leeann and her parents reached their car, her father turned his back on the others.

"Look, Leeann, there's Traci wandering away from her family," her mother said. "Go speak to her. Say you're sorry."

"And then what?"

"Say whatever comes to mind."

Leeann made a face. "No, I really don't want to, Mom."

Her mother tugged at Leeann's arm and together they turned back and approached Traci as she fired snowballs at a nearby tree. When Leeann's mother called to her, Traci brushed snow off her hands and lifted her bewildered-looking face. She folded into Helene's chest, pressing her face in the wide rabbit fur collar of her coat.

"We are so sorry, Traci."

"Sorry about what happened," Leeann muttered. She waited for a word or a gesture from her friend but got nothing. The three hunched together, shivering in the cold, until Traci ran to the waiting limousine.

"We shouldn't have talked to her." Leeann kicked snow in the air. "We made her feel worse. You made her feel worse, Mom."

"No, you showed you cared."

"We made her feel horrible." All the way home Leeann thought of Traci and wondered how she was going to return to school and make it through each day. She didn't talk to her mother, even when she turned around in her seat and offered Leeann a cherry Lifesaver.

Richard Bright started drinking beer as soon as they got home from church. Leeann retreated to her room. Her mind was a tangle of thoughts about her father running from the fire, the promise she'd made to him, and Traci's father's funeral. She felt as if she was going crazy having to keep so much inside.

When the bickering started, she thought, here we go again. She clenched her fists and her chest tightened, thinking of the night ahead. Her father's drinking led to fighting and that sometimes led to her mother getting hit. Why did they get married, she often wondered. Her mother once told her she married when she was eighteen to get out of an abusive foster home. Leeann's father was twenty-eight. He'd moved to New Hampshire from Canada to start an auto repair business with his uncle until he caught his uncle stealing the profits. After that, her parents moved from New Hampshire to Western Massachusetts to find work in the mills. Leeann pulled the bed covers over her head.

Later that night, Leeann's mother invited her to watch *The Saturday Night Movie* in the living room. "Your dad's dead asleep in the recliner." The program featured *The African Queen*. Katherine Hepburn's terror-filled face, covered with a suffocating cloud of small black flies, filled the television screen. Hepburn, playing Rose Sayer, cruising down the Bora River with Humphrey Bogart as Charlie Allnutt, swatted at the disgusting little critters. Leeann's mother let out a groan. To a twelve-year-old girl, the picture of insects hovering all over Rose's face was disgusting. It would, however, be something fascinating to talk about at school on Monday.

"This is cool, Mom. I love this gross stuff."

Leeann's father stirred in his chair. "Helene, get me a beer."

"You've had enough, Richard. Besides, you're out of work. You don't have money for beer."

And it began. "You should charge more for your flowers this spring. You're giving them away."

"Let's talk about you, Richard. You're the one who's been out of work a hell of a lot these past twelve years." She stood and headed toward the kitchen.

Leeann's stomach lurched when her father followed.

"I gave you a home, didn't I? Better than that foster place you grew up in."

Leeann cringed. She hated the way cruel remarks went hand in hand with her father's drinking.

Dishes slammed and cabinet drawers banged as her mother put away washed plates and silverware. "If you cared about the family, you'd go back to Drumlin's Garage and ask for your old job back."

"When I asked them for a raise, they laughed at me. No, I won't go back there. Richard Bright is no beggar."

Leeann recognized the familiar signs of disaster. Her mother called her husband selfish. Her father shouted that she never supported him. The wind rattled the living room windows and shook the sheets of plastic nailed to the window frames. Leeann tightened the belt to her bathrobe.

"The movie's starting again," Leeann called out.

Her father stood in the kitchen doorway, his voice calm. "I'm leaving town. The Hannahs said there's lots of construction jobs in San Francisco. I'm heading there next week."

"Construction! There's a steady job!"

Leeann never believed what her father said while drunk, but her mother seemed to take his words seriously.

"You can't leave us like this."

Her father walked into the living room. "You'll be glad to get rid of me."

Helene stood in the doorway between the kitchen and living room. "How can you afford to haul yourself cross-country? We have no money."

"Got lucky in poker."

Now she approached him, her face throbbing red. "You didn't have anything to do with that fire..."

"No," he bellowed.

"Why's Roland been calling every night?"

"He's wondering whether to rebuild. Wants my advice."

"There's more to this, I know it."

In the silence that followed, Leeann waited for her father to come clean about the fire, how the accident happened, how he'd kept quiet because he didn't want to get blamed for something he didn't do. Only her mother's words followed. "I hope to God you weren't involved."

Katherine Hepburn re-appeared on the television screen. Leeann put her hands over her ears. She faced the kitchen and fired her own ball of rage. "Quiet! Movie's on."

Her father flew across the living room and slammed the TV off button. The screen went black. Leeann's head snapped up, and she caught her father's face, contorted in fury.

"Shut up and go to your room," he screamed.

Leeann jumped up from the floor. She scrambled around, trying to get as far away from her father as she could before his hand came down on her. She ran to her room and closed the door, which squeaked in the silence of the house. She climbed under the covers thinking only about poor Katherine Hepburn and how she fought off the insects from around her face and how scared she must have been even though it was just a movie. And Leeann figured she must have been an awfully brave actress to let them put flying bugs all over her face, and she wondered if deep down she was really afraid or pretending to be afraid.

Leeann woke at sunrise. She put on her warmest fleece-lined blue jeans, old parka and gloves. She tucked her hair under a knit cap. The horizon at that hour appeared as a thick bar of gold. Above it, red-orange streaks nudged away smoke-colored clouds and a still dark sky. Stacked in a pile on her porch were thirty Sunday newspapers she would deliver on her bike to houses in the neighborhood. She'd been making money as a newspaper girl delivering papers seven days a week since she was nine. As she stuffed papers inside her canvas bag, she glimpsed the headline on page one of the *Berkshire Ridge Advocate*. Leeann stumbled onto the porch step, grabbed the railing, and sat down. She stared, holding her breath, at the headline: *Fire Marshall calls blaze at Mechanics Garage suspicious, possibly arson, investigation continues.*

CHAPTER 5

WESTERN MASSACHUSETTS, Berkshire Ridge
March, 1983
Leeann Bright, 12 years old

Dressed in her yellow slicker and boots, Leeann sloshed through puddles from the porch to her father's truck. She placed a soggy cardboard box full of books into the truck's bed and stepped out of the way so her father could add three suitcases, boots, and a sleeping bag. It was ten days after the fire.

"I want to go with you," she said, when he returned with his toolbox. "I want to see Hollywood and some movie stars. And Disneyland is there, too."

"You stay and keep your mother company. Help her open the nursery." His rough hand rested on the back of her head, reminding Leeann how smart her father was, how he could fix any car engine when no one else in town could.

Beneath a steady drizzle of rain, Leeann sat on the railing of the front porch. A spare tire, an empty can of automobile oil, and a rake littered the front yard. The milk carton she stood on to help her father repair his truck lay under the crab apple tree. Two abandoned golf clubs were covered in mud. There'd be no more golf practice with her dad. Leeann thought about life without him and prayed he'd change his mind. She realized she would have to drag the trash barrels to the sidewalk every Monday, and the broken post and rail fence would never be repaired. Gallon cans of paint—lemon meringue yellow—sat under the eaves. She knew for sure the house would never get painted lemon meringue yellow. The light bulb in the wall-mount lantern next to the front door had been dead for weeks and would stay that way. The rusty mailbox was swinging off its hinges.

Wind gusts swept across the yard, whipping and yanking holly bushes alongside the house. It was the kind of wind that bent tree branches and lifted puddles off the ground. The rain came down harder.

Leeann went into the living room and leafed through her Nancy Drew mystery books. Beside her, a metal bucket caught the water that leaked through the roof. The problem had gone on for so long her parents didn't seem to notice the sound of heavy drops landing in the bucket. They didn't seem to notice the bucket Leeann emptied each rainy night.

At the sound of the truck's engine, Leeann went out to the porch and called through the rain. "You said you'd have a surprise before you left."

"Almost forgot." He walked to the porch and handed her a shopping bag. Leeann pulled out a snow globe and a Boston Red Sox banner for her wall. Another time, she might have spun with joy over her gifts, but at that moment she felt no pleasure.

"I love these, Dad. Please…"

"No," he said, pulling his wallet from his pocket and checking its contents, then tucking it back inside his back pocket. Her father hurried toward his truck. "Now go see if your mother is all right." They said no good-byes.

She went inside and leaned the side of her face against her mother's closed bedroom door. "Mom, Dad's taking off now." When she got no response, she went to the front door and took in the bewildering sight of her father leaving. Pebbles of gravel danced like jumping beans in the driveway. Her father's blue hat and red hair faded as his truck turned left at the end of the driveway and disappeared into the shadow of Berkshire Ridge Mountain.

Leeann couldn't understand why he didn't take her along. She'd kept her promise. They were the only people on earth who knew the truth about the Mechanics Garage fire and why Norman Stylofski died. And she had studied her geography book and planned a route along the coasts of the Great Lakes. She'd hoped to drive through the Mid-western farmlands that looked like yellow and green rectangles and through the southwestern plains of white hazy dust. She pictured herself beside a eucalyptus tree on a cliff above the Pacific Ocean.

Leeann went to her room and pulled her brown, battered suitcase from under her bed. She rubbed her hand across its bumpy surface, opened it, and removed the clothes she'd packed the night before—short-sleeve tee-shirts, pants, sweatshirt, underwear, socks, toothbrush—and put them back in her bureau drawer.

For the rest of the afternoon, she lost herself in a game she played with her two-dozen miniature lead figures of 15th century soldiers with their coat-of-arms and lances. They were four inches tall, and she'd painted many of them with the help of her father. She'd found them at a yard sale and asked her father to buy them for her. She divided them into two families and named each one. When she was through playing, she lined them up on a shelf on her bookcase, knowing they'd be there when she got into bed every night and when she woke up every morning.

CHAPTER 6

EASTERN MASSACHUSETTS, Boston and surrounding suburbs
1998

Guarded?! Where does Traci get off calling her guarded? If anyone's guarded, it's Traci, terrified that her Boston friends will find out everyone back home thinks her drunk father died in a fire he started. That's guarded.

Leeann was fuming when, orchid in hand, she said goodbye to Traci on her front stoop. There was a catch in Traci's voice when she said, "Be careful driving home." Her eyes had a faraway look. Her mouth turned down at the corners.

Leeann pushed her anger aside. "I'm sorry about you and Jimmy, and I'm sorry I won't go with you next week."

Traci nodded and waved goodbye.

It was three o'clock in the afternoon. The skies darkened and rain began falling once again. As she drove, Leeann's mind wandered to Josh Wilson and his anonymous note. Gripping the wheel, she thought the Berkshire Ridge police might soon be examining incriminating evidence. The muscles in her neck tightened. Fifteen years ago there was no DNA testing. Investigations stalled. There were no video cameras outside the Mechanics Garage. Today, investigators find a hair on a doorknob and within days they can tell whose head it belonged to. What if her father left a strand of hair?

A watery mist cut visibility, and thick slush covered the rural road. Leeann focused on a bicyclist ahead, his head down and body covered in clear plastic sheeting. He was riding in the middle of the lane, and Leeann hovered behind him. The oncoming lane to Leeann's left was clear—there was hardly anyone on the road that afternoon—and she pulled into it. She passed the biker, moved back in to her lane, and checked her rear view mirror. The biker appeared to be a young boy, a teenager, maybe. Bare red hands gripped wet handlebars. The front wheel of his bike slid back and forth on flooding pavement. Now he was all over the road. Leeann slowed when her car began skidding, but regained control, and fighting the wind, kept the car in her lane. Needing to concentrate, she turned off the radio. A thud jolted the car, and she slammed on the brakes. Oh my god, the biker. She looked at her rear view mirror. Where's the biker? She saw no one. Her heart seized.

She swung around to look out the rear window, hoping to see the boy walking, running, pushing a bike along the road. Trembling, Leeann opened her car door. Through the battering rain, she raced to the boy, lying motionless in a pool of icy water. Leeann placed two fingers on his soaking wet wrist. She felt a pulsing artery. The boy's color was good. He was taking in air. Leeann grabbed his shoulder. "Hey, are you okay? Hey! Hey!" She shook harder.

The boy's eyes fluttered open. "Oh, my hip," he said. His corduroys and sweater were soaked. "I shouldn't have tried to pass you." He placed his hand on his helmet. "Did I put a dent in your car?"

"Yeah, but at least you're okay." Water drizzled down their faces. The clear plastic sheeting that had covered the boy floated down Covey Road and got stuck on a leafless branch of a burning bush. "I'll drive you home." She helped him up and placed the bike with its bent front wheel in her trunk. She stared at the boy in the passenger seat, fighting visions of him crushed under her car's tires or lying on the pavement with his head cracked open.

"Drive straight and turn after the industrial park," the boy said, pointing.

"What's your name?"

"Eric Downey."

Eric Downey didn't make eye contact with Leeann. His face took on a scowl. Leeann told herself that the boy was alive and that's all that mattered. Thank God the accident wasn't her fault. Then why did she have a steel grip on the steering wheel? Why couldn't she breathe normally? Why was there sweat above her lip and across her forehead? Eric flopped his head against the passenger window.

"Are you hurt anywhere besides your hip, Eric? Anything bothering you?"

"My mom," he muttered.

"Your mom will be happy you're okay, and you'll find someone to fix that front wheel," Leeann replied. The boy responded with a smirk and a straight-ahead glare.

Eric's house was a run-down structure with a roof patched with mismatched shingles. A rain gutter dangled off one corner of the house. Trash barrels blocked the front door. It was nearly three months past Christmas, yet the fence encircling the house displayed gold garlands and a Christmas wreath. A gigantic peppermint cane and yellow colored balls with a metallic glimmer adorned the windows of the house. As Leeann lifted Eric's bike from her trunk, she noticed strings of green and blue Christmas lights wound in web-like fashion through the bare branches of the single towering maple tree in the front yard. "My mom keeps the decorations up 'til around August," he said, with a what-can-you-do shrug.

Inside the house, Mrs. Downey, a thin woman with a flaming orange buzz cut, hugged and chastised her son for the accident. A statue of a Buddha rested on a bookcase. Paintings of Ganesha, the Hindu god of prosperity, stared down from three sides of the room. Leeann thought she could have been standing at a shrine or an ancient temple. Mrs. Downey apologized to Leeann for what happened. She had to have the name and address of the fine woman who'd rescued her son, and Leeann obliged. She wrote her address and phone number on the index card Mrs. Downey handed her.

"What do you do for work?"

"I'm a certified public accountant," Leeann answered.

"And how old are you, Leeann?"

"Twenty-seven."

"You look like one of those pretty TV anchors on the news. Look at that gorgeous long red hair of yours."

"Well, I appreciate the compliment, thank you." But she didn't think Mrs. Downey heard her reply. The whistle of a teakettle called her out of the room, and as Leeann watched her leave, she noticed a five-piece drum set with cymbals in the hallway and asked Eric if he played them. "No, they're my mom's. She plays them when she gets mad, which is like every day." He whispered the last half of his remark, but Leeann heard it clearly.

"I'd like to make you some tea," Mrs. Downey said, returning.

"No thank you, I just wanted to make sure Eric was okay. I could drive him to the emergency room, if you'd like."

"Don't worry, he gets banged up worse than this on the football field." She opened the front door and thanked Leeann for her kindness. Leeann sprinted through the sleet, across the yard. A huge gust snapped pine branches in half over her head, dropping them in scattered heaps on the lawn, narrowly missing her. Served her right, she thought, for driving around in a Nor'easter.

CHAPTER 7

EASTERN AND WESTERN MASSACHUSETTS
1998

Traci pleaded all week for Leeann to join her on the trip to Berkshire Ridge. After listening to a half dozen of Traci's voice mail messages, in a moment of weakness, Leeann relented. Her affection for Traci overruled her conflicted feelings about hearing more about the new so-called evidence. She'd looked out for her friend since childhood. She wouldn't stop now.

The trip to the western part of the state would take two hours. Traci picked up Leeann in Concord. They'd been driving only a few minutes when Leeann leaned back in her seat. "I forgot to tell you that I almost killed your neighbor on Covey Road last week. A kid." Leeann explained that the boy, on a bike, plowed into her car, that he'd ended up on the ground and Leeann thought he was a goner. "I drove him home, 'though he didn't seem at all grateful for the help. Do you know Eric Downey?"

"He mowed my lawn last summer. Nice kid, but the mother's crazy. She gets into a lot of car accidents, if you know what I mean."

"A scammer?"

"Some people think so. Hope you didn't talk to her."

"Well…briefly."

"Stay far away from that woman. She's bad news. I'm serious."

At eleven o'clock they entered Berkshire Ridge. Traci turned onto Mechanics Garage Drive and parked. She pointed from the driver's seat. "My father died right over there in that spot. I'm getting out. C'mon." She walked up to Mechanics Garage and placed her hand on a glass pane. Leeann stayed inside the truck, rifling through her backpack looking for a bottle of water. Traci stepped back and shook her head from side to side. "It's the same one-story steel and glass building that's been here at least a dozen years. They replaced the old one after the fire," she called out to Leeann. She put her fist over her mouth.

Leeann thought of getting out of the truck and comforting Traci, but instead, hit the horn and pointed to her watch.

Traci revved the engine and pulled away from the site. "After Roland Barnes died a few years ago, new owners modernized the main entrance with these new doors that shoot up when you bring your car within inches of them." She shielded her eyes from the sun. "Those doors are cheap vinyl, but they painted them to look like a wood grain design."

Leeann didn't care what the Mechanics Garage looked like, now or then. She wished she were home working on her miniature terrarium with begonia and creeping fig and English ivy. She should have been repotting her Christmas cactus.

"You think Josh is going to ask me how my family coped with losing my dad?"

"I can't say," Leeann said, not wanting to be drawn into a discussion about Norm Stylofski.

"Do you think he'll ask me what my dad was like?"

"I'm not a journalist, Traci. I don't know what he's going to ask. I think he's using you to get a front-page story and sell papers. Why else would he dredge up painful memories? It's cruel."

"Maybe he'll put my picture on the front-page." Her eyes opened wide.

"Are you doing this interview to become a Berkshire Ridge celebrity?"

"Course not. I want to talk about my dad." She tugged at the corner of her wrinkled hoodie.

Leeann had been short with Traci and now she cringed. "Sorry Traci, I'm being a jerk. It's this town. Don't you remember when we were kids and everyone who lived here seemed trapped? They were poor or uneducated or down on their luck."

"I hate the memories too," Traci said. "But I have to come back to visit my sister once in a while."

Leeann remembered that Traci's mother and two of her sisters moved to Tennessee years ago after their house went to foreclosure. Her sister Vivian remained in town.

A half mile from the Garage on a busy two-lane road, Traci approached the Blue Iris Nursery, which Leeann's mother had owned, and where Leeann worked all through middle school and high school. "Go slow," Leeann said. It was closed for winter. Leeann couldn't shake the flood of emotion. Tears formed at the edges of her eyes, and she was surprised at her reaction. "Had the best time of my life working here with my mom." A sign with painted daffodils said, 'Be back in spring.'

Leeann realized she'd made a colossal mistake agreeing to the interview. She felt as if a boulder was sitting on her chest. As Traci accelerated, Leeann thought about her tendency to let Traci talk her into doing things she didn't want to do. Last year she got roped into deep-sea fishing and spent the afternoon hurling over the railing.

"Drop me off at Loden's," Leeann said.

"You're not doing the interview?"

"No, I can't let you talk me into doing things I don't want to do."

Traci gripped the steering wheel and stared straight ahead. The cheerfulness that had brightened her face dissolved into a scowl. The silence in the car, the tension, caused Leeann to slump back in her seat and stare out the passenger window. By the time they passed the Sudbury Cemetery on Falls Road, Traci was talking again. She asked Leeann if she wanted to pay a visit to her mother's grave. Leeann reminded Traci that her mother wasn't buried in Berkshire Ridge, but that her ashes had been scattered on the Piscataqua River in New Hampshire where her mother grew up.

"Me, John Wicker, who was my mom's assistant manager at the nursery, if you remember, Coach Maddie and her husband piled into the car and drove all the way to the coast for her ceremony. And with my mother's love of flowers, none of us thought to bring a friggin' one to throw into the river with her ashes. It didn't occur to me to reach down along the fence at the nursery and grab some irises. That bothered me for a long time."

"You were seventeen, for crying out loud." Traci reached over and touched her friend's arm. "Your mom was real nice. She showed interest in me."

"Your mom was nice, too."

"Your mom ran a business. My mom had no initiative to do anything. She waited for men to take care of her. That didn't work out."

"Sounds like she was depressed, Traci."

"Possibly. My house was crazy, that's for sure." She turned into Loden's parking lot and pulled up to the back door. Leeann jumped out. She lifted her backpack from the floor. "Don't let Josh get any ideas about coming back here to interview me."

"Don't worry. God, you worry so much."

Leeann wandered through Loden's Family Tavern, now modernized and called Loden's Bistro and Grill. She hadn't been inside in over twelve years. The dining room was noisy, brimming with young people, families, couples, and teenagers. The stuffed trout that had been mounted over the bar was gone. Gone too, were the pool table and country music and the black and white checkered tile floor. Will Simpson was no longer bar manager at Loden's. He moved to Key West after his wife ran off with another man, according to Traci, who kept up with the town's gossip through her sister. Leeann took a booth in a corner and ordered iced tea. She had no appetite for food, although she did scan the menu. A recent issue of *Glamour* kept her company. With time to kill after two glasses of iced tea, Leeann wandered through Loden's parking lot and onto the road. She walked a quarter mile to shake off her restlessness and clear her head. She headed back to Loden's after Traci passed her on the road, curious to know who her passenger was.

A clot of anger lodged in Leeann's throat when Josh Wilson, six feet tall and bean-pole skinny, emerged from Traci's truck. Goddamn it, Traci, Leeann thought. Josh grabbed Leeann's hand. "Great to see you again, Leeann. Long time no see." Leeann forced a half smile. "Same here." She wouldn't look at Traci and reluctantly agreed to drinks inside Loden's before she and Traci got back on the road.

The conversation centered on Josh's new job as editor of the *Advocate* and about the changing face of Berkshire Ridge. New townhouses, the new state college, and an expansion of the Berkshire Ridge Hospital, now called the Western New England Medical Center, had brought young people to the area. He talked about their former friends who'd left town and never returned. He didn't ask Leeann and Traci about themselves.

Traci occupied herself drumming her fingers on the table and rearranging the silverware. Leeann suspected the interview with Josh didn't go well. She wanted to tell Traci she could have predicted that.

"I was telling Traci that I'd forgotten all about the Mechanics Garage fire," Josh began. "But two weeks ago, I received an anonymous letter, or rather, a note, and it gave me the idea to do this anniversary story. When I read it to Traci, she said that I had to read it to you in person." Josh took a white piece of paper from his jacket pocket and read:

Mechanic's Garage fire, 1983—ask Richard Bright what happened.

Traci's eyes darted around the room.

Leeann looked up at Josh. "Will you read that again?"

Josh's monotone sliced through every other sound around Leeann: her heart knocking against her chest, the ambulance siren screaming in the distance, Traci's heavy breathing. When Josh finished reading the note a second time, he and Traci stared at Leeann.

"It must have been some prankster sending rubbish like that," Leeann said.

The two continued to stare, as if they hadn't heard Lee-ann's words.

"Maybe someone had it in for my dad."

"Who?" Josh asked.

"How should I know? Maybe it's not referring to my dad."

"Of course they're referring to your dad. He worked there," Traci said. "And not for nothing, he left town a few days after the fire."

Leeann felt heat on her face. "The note says 'ask him,' it doesn't say he's responsible for the fire."

"Don't get defensive," Traci admonished.

"I don't like how you two are glaring at me, like I owe you an explanation."

"We're puzzled, like you probably are," Josh added.

Leeann pushed aside her Cosmopolitan, making room for the plate of nachos Josh ordered. But all she saw was a plate of yellow grease, and when Josh and Traci dug in, she sat back and gulped the last few swallows of her drink. Her stomach turned with a familiar sourness, as it did at work when she was about to miss important deadlines or was called to the VP's office for questioning about her handling of a disgruntled client.

"The place here looks good since they did it over, huh?" Leeann said. "The new floor and lighting? Why are you both still staring at me?"

"No one's saying your dad did anything wrong," Josh said. "Maybe someone told him something."

Leeann ordered another Cosmopolitan. "You're both making a federal case out of something some jokester did."

Traci asked Leeann if she would pass the calamari and Leeann shoved the plate toward her so hard that she knocked over Traci's water glass.

"Sorry, didn't mean that. This is just upsetting."

Josh continued, "Well yes, the letter is likely a scam, but let's consider for just a moment that it could be true."

"Why? Why should we consider that?" Leeann felt the temperature rising in the room. She wiped sweat from her forehead.

"Because if you'd stop being so defensive, maybe you could help," he said.

"I was twelve. What help do you think I can give you? You two are getting on my nerves."

"Leeann, please..." Traci began.

"The two of you and this conversation are pissing me off."

They came out of Loden's zipping up their jackets, Josh and Traci saying how good it was to have gotten together. Leeann seethed at being ambushed. A jolt of panic washed through her. After all these years, why would someone dig up the Mechanics Garage fire? It's over and done. She told herself she wasn't going to deal with the note, Traci or Josh.

"You putting the contents of the note in your story, Josh?" Leeann asked.

"Course not," he said. "Can't be verified." He told Traci he'd get his own ride back to the newspaper.

Leeann's feet crunched on a layer of frozen snow covering the grass in front of Loden's. She wanted to leave the whole dreary town behind and never come back. They sat silent in the truck as Traci swerved out of the parking lot, nearly hitting a Volvo. The light at the intersection turned green, and she sped toward the highway.

"You know, I did think it was strange how you backed out of the interview at the last minute." Traci looked straight ahead.

"You mean the interview I never wanted to do?" Leeann fixed her eyes on Traci. "The note is bullshit, Traci, bullshit."

"Someone went to the trouble of sending it."

"How do I know *you* didn't send it?"

"Leeann, you're sounding psychotic. You think I'm trying to put the blame on your father instead of mine?"

"Someone sent a note. What am I supposed to think?"

"Nothing, but it sure would be nice to be able to ask your dad if he knows what that note means."

"Great. Why don't you do that, Traci. Why don't you find my dad and ask him. And isn't it too bad we can't ask *your* dad what happened that night."

A gasp slipped from Traci's lips.

"I'm sorry I said that, Traci. I had too many Cosmos. I'm really sorry. I didn't mean it. What you went through was traumatic." She whispered under her breath, "My childhood wasn't a church picnic either."

Traci turned on the radio. They listened to music for the two-hour ride home.

In front of her house, Leeann rubbed her hand along her forehead, trying to massage away a headache. She got out of Traci's car, slammed the passenger door shut, and gave a half-hearted, get-out-of-here wave to Traci, who roared away. Leeann walked across the yard toward her back door over the lawn, still soft and damp from melting snow. The rear porch was lit by a single bare bulb, which protruded from the house above the back door. She stood on the porch as she searched for her key, the full moonlight spilling a glow onto the backyard. It illuminated the snow and a set of shovels leaning against the shed, and cast a golden hue on it all, and on the police cruiser pulling into her driveway.

"Something wrong?" she said to the officer stepping out of his cruiser. The officer asked Leeann to identify herself, asked if she'd been to Medina the week before, and if she'd been in an accident with a biker. Leeann nodded yes to the questions.

"A Karen Downey of Medina says you veered your car into her son on his bike and caused him to be thrown in to the street. Kid was badly injured. Says you left the scene of the accident, but after fifteen minutes you returned and helped the boy home."

Leeann's voice shook. "That's not how the accident happened, and Mrs. Downey...she's lying."

"Her son corroborated everything."

"Sure, he's lying for his mother." Leeann threw her hands in the air, almost hitting the officer in the arm. "Kids will lie for their parents."

He didn't flinch. "I've a summons for you to appear in court on April fifteenth.

Her head spun. "Officer, I believe Karen Downey has made me a target in a scam." He handed Leeann an envelope. She stared straight ahead, toward the neighbor's yard, at the tip of the tallest pine tree swaying in the wind.

CHAPTER 8

WESTERN MASSACHUSETTS, Berkshire Ridge
April, 1983
Leeann Bright, 12 years old

Dear Dad:
The Fire Chief says the Mechanics Garage fire was an accident. Mr. Barnes is going to tear down the old garage and build a brand new one. Your old job will be waiting. We don't have to keep our secret anymore. You can come home now.
Love,
Your daughter Leeann

Leeann wrote the letter sitting at her desk and stored it in her top bureau drawer. It was the last Monday of April, four weeks after her father left, and there'd been no official report on the cause of the Mechanics Garage fire. Each morning since then, she'd scanned the newspaper, searching for news that the Mechanics Garage fire had been declared an accident. When that day came, she would mail her letter to her dad. Leeann wasn't sure where to mail it, but decided to tackle that problem when it was time. Until then, she would eat her buttered toast and check each page of the newspaper before her paper route, before leaving for school every day.

Traci Stylofski knocked on the Bright's back door that Monday evening after dinner.

Startled to see her classmate, Leeann shifted her weight from side to side.

"Want to go for a bike ride?"

"I don't think my mom will let me go out now." Leeann had played softball with Traci last summer, but she'd never hung out with her on a regular basis. She did know that Traci's friends had been avoiding her at school. Recently, Leeann told her mother that Traci was eating lunch in the cafeteria alone. Her mother had shaken her head. She'd said that kids often didn't know how to talk to a girl whose father died, that they didn't know the right thing to say. Leeann's mother told her that kids were afraid of Traci's sadness and afraid of their own sadness, as well. Leeann had said she understood and added, "After lunch today, before anyone came back to class, I left half of my Skybar on Traci's desk—the nougat and caramel parts." Leeann had earned an extra big hug from her mother that day.

"Just a ride over to Walden's Park?" Traci asked.

Leeann shook her head.

Helene Bright was putting away dishes. Through the screen door, she greeted Traci. "You can go for a quick ride, Leeann," she said, drying her hands on her apron.

The two girls rode to the lagoon at Walden's and parked on the footbridge at its highest point. Leeann leaned over the bridge railing and studied the body of water, which twisted like a vine through the park. Traci checked out one of her tires that seemed to be losing air. After a few minutes, they got back on their bikes and rode. They cut through the center of town. Traci led the way over the railroad tracks, past the Lutheran Church. She rode to the strip of stores that made up downtown and stopped in front of Bob's Toy Store.

Traci pressed her forehead against the store window. "I never owned a model kit. Sure would like to build that clipper ship."

Leeann leaned against the window too. "That's a double planked Canadian schooner, not a clipper."

Traci looked puzzled, then said she knew that but had forgotten. "What's that one?" she asked, pointing.

"An ancient Greek fishing boat."

Traci hopped back on her bike. "Cool. I'll race you."

They rode around Berkshire Ridge until twilight. Tall pines looked like silhouettes against the slate blue sky. At Waters Field they collapsed on the ground at second base. They looked up at the sky and the faintness of the moon. Leeann's thoughts wandered to a time earlier that day, to questions she'd gotten from kids in homeroom. *Why did your dad move so far away? When's he coming home? Why didn't he take you and your mom?* Traci didn't ask about her father, either at school or during their ride, and Leeann adored her for that.

Traci broke the silence. "People keep saying my dad started the fire."

Her voice startled Leeann. "Your dad didn't start the fire. It must have been an accident." Leeann got up on her elbows and turned to Traci. "You want to go to the fire station and ask the chief about the investigation?"

A grin spread across Traci's face. "I'd like that."

"Meet me at 3:00 tomorrow at the bench in front of the war memorial across from the fire station." Leeann got up from the ground, brushing dirt off the back of her shirt. "I have to get going." She couldn't wait to hear what the Chief had to say.

CHAPTER 9

EASTERN MASSACHUSETTS, Boston and surrounding suburbs
1998

Leeann met Traci every Monday evening after work at the Exeter Fitness Club in downtown Boston for an hour of tennis and a workout. They hadn't spoken in over a week, since their trip to Berkshire Ridge and argument on the drive home. Leeann didn't go to the gym on Monday after the fight. She'd been fuming over what had happened at Loden's. She doubted Traci showed up either. But tonight she waited on a lumpy sofa in the lobby, pondering the possibility that the argument signaled a crack in their friendship. She regretted making the cruel comment about Traci's dead father. Now, the thought of her friend storming out of her life in a stony grudge made her sick to her stomach.

Finally, she spotted her coming through the door.

Traci held her sports bag in one hand, a cup of coffee in the other and greeted Leeann with a mumble. "I didn't get the promotion to construction manager."

"I thought they were going to hand you that job on a platter."

Traci looked pale, and her strong, athletic body was hunched over as if claiming defeat. "They said it was because I didn't have management experience." She shook her head. "Real reason is the empty suits didn't want a woman on the management team."

"You've got to fight this."

"I'm thinking of quitting."

"I know you're crushed, but don't quit your job."

"Let's play. I can't think right now."

On the court, arms flailing, Traci missed the ball over and over, and when she made contact, smashed the ball with such fury it went out of bounds. After losing her third game, she called it quits.

They decided to skip their workout in favor of drinking Margaritas in the glassed-in Man in the Moon Café, overlooking the Olympic-size swimming pool.

Leeann spoke first. "I owe you an apology."

"Back at ya."

"Really, let me finish. I never should have made that comment about your dad."

"Forget it. It wasn't my finest moment either."

"I wasn't sure you'd show up. The thought of losing you made me sick."

"Don't get all emotional on me, please." She looked away. "After I graduated from college," Traci began, "I fell into this horrendous depression and," she paused and looked down, "I thought about suicide." She stroked her hair, which looked as unkempt as her clothes. "I'd drive over the Tobin Bridge and think how easy it'd be for me to stop the car and take a leap into that frigid Atlantic. And when those idiots told me I didn't get the promotion, I began thinking about that bridge."

"You're scaring me, Traci. I mean it's just a fucking promotion." Leeann signaled to the waiter for another round of Margaritas. "You're not serious, are you?"

"Course not. I'd never do that to Jimmy, who, at this point, wouldn't care."

"Not true, you jerk, but stay away from bridges for a while."

"Hey, I build them. All I know is construction, and I'm a failure at that."

"Traci, you look like hell. You've got to get a grip."

"No promotion, no husband. You know, the reason Jimmy left is because he wants to have kids and I don't. I'd *really* be a failure at that."

"Not true," Leeann said. She hadn't seen that comment coming.

"After my dad died, what was left of my family was so screwed up," Traci said. "My mother had all these boyfriends, who were drunks and addicts, always high on something. And God they fought. Mom was always ending up in the emergency room with a black eye or swollen jaw. Those assholes. At home, life was a free for all, no rules, no schedules, no discipline."

"So you'll know what not to do as a parent." She looked away from Traci, fixing her eyes on the purple walls.

"You know, Leeann, it's bugged me since I was twelve years old. What if my father had quit drinking, gotten a job, and cared for us? Everything would have been different for us kids and my mom."

"Traci, where are you going with this?"

"I'm upset with myself. All these years have passed, and I've never made an attempt to clear my father's name. He can't do it. I'm his only chance."

"Traci, it's been years. Time to move on."

"Nope, can't do that. It's affected my marriage and my self-esteem. When I didn't get the promotion, I thought, 'They know I'm the kid whose father started the fire that killed him.' I don't want to be that kid anymore." Traci paused, avoiding Leeann's eyes. "I'm going to find out who set the fire that killed my dad. That note Josh showed us, I think it's real. I'm going to find your dad in California." There was a lifting of energy in her voice. "I'm betting he knows who set the fire and why."

A boulder-sized knot formed in Leeann's gut. "Whoa, do I have some say?"

"You're going to help me."

"No, I'm not going to help you. I have no interest in seeing my father. I've absolutely no feelings for him. Besides, are you prepared to find out that maybe your dad did set the fire?" Leeann rubbed the table with her hand, as though flicking crumbs aside.

"He didn't. Everyone thinks he did. I'm going to prove them wrong."

"Well don't drag me into this. My father walked away from me fifteen years ago. I let it go. You should too." Traci's presence was wearing on Leeann. "I can't help you. Sorry."

Leeann saw the disapproval on Traci's face. She saw disapproval everywhere—in the numbers scribbled on the check in front of her, in the moon faces on the wall, in the wilting Alstroemeria sitting in the silver bud vase on their table.

"Anyway, I'm preoccupied with my court case," Leeann began.

"What court case?"

"Your neighbor, Mrs. Friggin' Fruitcake Scam Artist is bringing me to court for swerving into her kid on his bike and leaving the scene of an accident in which such kid was seriously injured."

Traci's face grew serious as Leeann told her how she'd have to find an attorney, and hoped she wouldn't have to stand trial for her alleged criminal behavior.

"Ben will help me."

"Ben?! He's the worst choice of attorney for you."

Leeann threw some dollar bills on the table. "I wouldn't trust anyone else."

"You're supposed to be moving on, not setting yourself up to get hurt again."

Leeann didn't respond. In the parking lot, she climbed into her car and rolled down her window. "Hey, how did Josh's article turn out?"

"Real good. It was about my family, how difficult life was for us after the fire. Josh interviewed some firefighters who were there that night. Story reminded people that the cause of the fire has never been discovered."

Ben excelled at being an attorney. He was Leeann's only choice for legal help. Despite Traci's words of caution, the next morning she hurried a client out of her office, sat at her desk, and sent Ben an email: *I've been summoned to court. Can you represent me?* He emailed back: *Of course*. Leeann's heart raced at the response. Those two words stirred memories and emotions.

Ben was her first real love. They'd met at her colleague's wedding reception in Vermont over two years before. Leeann was attracted to the tall, dark haired disc jockey the moment they made eye contact. He had large teeth set in a perpetual smile. She learned he was an attorney by day, and on weekends he traded his ties and white shirts for a diamond earring and a day's growth of beard to perform at weddings. His hands bounced on make-believe drums in front of him, and he nodded nonstop to keep beat with the music.

They made eye contact again after the cutting of the wedding cake. He called her the next day. The romance blossomed that first year of dating, and he moved into her house in Concord. They were inseparable.

After the breakup in November, Leeann didn't go to her office for two days. She stayed in bed and listened to classical CD's. Dishes piled up on her kitchen counter. Her bed went unmade for a week. She physically ached over the loss of him. Maybe she shouldn't have pushed so hard for marriage. He told her he loved her, but after two years, he was not ready to make a commitment. It was like a sick joke, Leeann told Traci. She was in love with a wedding DJ who wanted no part of marriage.

He needed more time he'd told her. Consumed with rejection, she demanded he move out. On a wind-driven Friday afternoon, a week before Thanksgiving, he packed his clothes, books, dishes, and furniture and moved to a rented apartment in Boston. Leeann felt like her twelve-year-old self, watching him drive away on a cold, rainy day.

CHAPTER 10

EASTERN MASSACHUSETTS, Boston and surrounding suburbs
1998

"I've never seen a judge so nasty," Ben said, leading Leeann out of Medina District Court. He held open the double glass doors. She stepped in front of him, thrusting out her hips like a runway model.

"You were great when it was your turn to talk, Ben." It was the third compliment she'd given him that morning. "I loved the way you interrupted the judge." Leeann knew that some of Ben's colleagues found him brash, a trait she'd always liked about him.

"I tried being tactful, but Your Honor thought I was challenging her holy authority. That's when she got all sarcastic on me."

Leeann pleaded 'no contest' to the charges against her. Her preference had been to plead 'not guilty,' opening her up to a possible conviction, so Ben advised against that.

"All you need is some sweet-faced boy testifying that you were speeding in the rain, or fiddling with the radio, and that you plowed into him and left the scene. Also, the police-prosecutor told me he didn't believe your story. He believed the kid and his mother."

They walked through the courthouse parking lot. Ben slipped off his suit jacket. It was noon, and the day had warmed since early morning.

"Unbelievable," Leeann said, stopping and letting a car pass. "This kook, Downey, is making up fiction so she can get money out of me."

"Happens all the time." Ben checked his watch. "What's different about this case is that she's gotten her son to lie."

Leeann cranked her head toward him. "Maybe he has no choice."

"It's disgusting." Ben shook his head. "You wonder how this kid's life is going to turn out."

Leeann blinked twice. "You wonder." She climbed into the passenger seat of his Volkswagon, remembering the hundreds of times they'd driven to restaurants, beaches, movies, concerts and musicals. She smoothed the fabric of her camel-colored coat and smiled.

"Your gardening lessons have stuck with me, you know," he began. "I bought a couple pots of cyclamen from a client who owns a nursery and managed to keep them alive."

Leeann was lifted by his words, by his inference she was still part of his life.

"Have you heard of the Silver Sword Nursery in Haverhill?"

Leeann shook her head.

"It's going to foreclosure. I might need to consult with you on nurseries."

He needed her, she thought. He trusted her. She beamed.

"Leeann, I'd like to take you to dinner."

"I don't think that's a good idea for either of us, Ben, unless you've reconsidered making a commitment."

"It's just dinner."

"I don't understand you, Ben. Maybe you have issues. I don't know."

"I don't have issues, Leeann. I'm a normal guy not ready to get married."

Tension rose in the car and accompanied them all the way to Acton.

At the train station, he pulled to the curb and turned off the engine. "Hey, I'm running the Boston Marathon on Monday with some of my buddies from work. Come cheer me on. Please?"

Leeann pressed her lips together and shook her head.

Ben remained in his car while she got out and walked to the driver's side window.

She blinked back tears. "I appreciate your being my lawyer for a day," she said, slipping off the curb and hopping back onto the sidewalk. She swallowed the lump in her throat. "It was good seeing you." Her voice betrayed her and cracked. "I have to get my train."

"Let me take you to that place you love on Beacon Hill," he said.

She waved him off.

"I'm still crazy about you," he said. "We were good together." He extended his arm in her direction, and she backed away.

"But not good enough for a future together."

He pounded his fist on the steering wheel.

Leeann walked off. She wanted to hurt him, wanted to lie and say she was seeing someone, and the relationship was serious. She wanted to tell him her new boyfriend was a TWA pilot with homes in the Bahamas and New York City, and that he drove a Porsche. It would have been a game. The height of immaturity.

Leeann made it to work a little after one o'clock. Her office was on the eighteenth floor with a wall of windows offering a view of the ever-changing sky and Boston skyline. When she interviewed for the job at Coopers six years earlier, it was not so much the job she was hoping to land—there were an abundance of accounting firms in the city—but that view of Boston. For the past six years, she relished sitting at her desk and watching planes take off from Logan Airport in the distance. The Custom House was in clear view, as were the ships that filled the harbor and the new luxury hotels along the skyline.

Darlene Summers stopped her at the elevator. "Leeann, hi, you missed our staff meeting this morning."

Leeann stared right through her. She didn't recall having a meeting scheduled.

"And your new client waited for you for an hour, then left."

Leeann wrinkled her brow. "Thanks, Darlene."

Later, her manager, McVey, grim-faced, stuck his head in Leeann's office and told her she'd missed a report deadline. Leeann closed the door behind him. She put her head on the desk, and squeezed her eyes shut. She had screwed up. Maybe she should have accepted Ben's dinner invitation.

CHAPTER 11

WESTERN MASSACHUSETTS, Berkshire Ridge
April, 1983
Leeann Bright, 12 years old

Chief Stan Gantry gripped his suspenders with both hands, leaned back in his chair, and stared at Leeann. "Bright," he said. "Your family owns the nursery over on Woodstock."

"My mom does," Leeann said. She dropped her gaze to an ashtray and a half-smoked cigar teetering on the edge of the metal desk.

"How can I help you, Leeann Bright?"

Leeann fiddled with her hands. She had waited on the bench for Traci for an hour, baking in the sun, but Traci never showed up. Tired and sweating, Leeann had summoned her courage, walked into the fire station, and found a firefighter repacking a hose on a fire truck. "May I speak to the Chief?"

Now, she struggled to get out her words. "When are you going to know what started the fire at Mechanics Garage?" She sat forward in her chair and rambled. "I think it started by accident. Bad wiring. Or maybe someone lit a candle and forgot about it and it fell over. And then there were all those rags and paint fumes. That can cause a fire."

The chief moved his hands up his forehead and through his hair. "You writing a paper for school?"

"No."

"How old are you?"

"Twelve."

"I don't get many visits from twelve year olds."

Leeann shrugged.

"Why so interested in the cause of the fire?"

"My friend Traci, she was supposed to be here today, her father died in it. She doesn't want everyone blaming her dad." Stacks of papers littered the floor. Three waste baskets overflowed with crumpled milk cartons. Two file cabinet drawers had been pulled out all the way and left in that position. A bottle of pink antacid sat on a bookcase. This was not an organized man. This was not a man who could solve problems, she thought. "We, I mean my friend, has to know for sure it was an accident."

"I'm sorry for your friend. Terrible tragedy," the chief said.

"Can't you tell me when you'll figure it out?"

His tone turned condescending. "These investigations take a long time. We're working at it. The police are looking over evidence, too, Louann. Is it Louann?"

"Leeann."

"Yes, Leeann." The chief tucked his cigar in the corner of his mouth and pulled his hefty body up from his chair. "Tell your friend to be patient." He gestured toward the door. "I've got work to do now."

Leeann's face flushed red at the dismissal. She wanted the chief to state without hesitation that the fire had been an accident so she could feel normal again.

The chief's final words took her by surprise. "You're a good friend to Traci."

No, she was not a good friend. She told lies to Traci and now she lied to the fire chief. She wanted nothing more than to confess her secret to her mother. She didn't like seeing herself as a liar to the police, to Traci, to the whole town, really.

On her bike, a slow burn tore at her insides. She pedaled faster, directionless. She crossed the Berkshire Ridge town line and entered picturesque, historic Claremont, where birch trees and evergreens lined the streets, and residents' front lawns looked like green velvet. She rode all the way to Hilton's Pond and found herself alone in the woods. At the edge of the pond, she sat on a broken, dead tree and studied the pattern of ridges on the log beneath her. She dared herself to scream out loud, relieving herself of her secret. *My father started the fire at Mechanics Garage.* The thought sent shivers through her torso and down her arms. She remained quiet, however.

Leeann cranked her head upward, toward the boulder that was at least two stories high. If she were able to climb to the top of it and throw her bike in the air, it would sink to the bottom of Hilton's Pond. She could tell everyone her bike was stolen at Morse's Strawberry Farm where she'd gone to pet the baby goats they kept in a pen for the public to view. Yes, it happened there. She'd gone into the shop to buy strawberries, came out, bike gone. It was a cool bike and she loved it. Her parents gave it to her the Christmas before the fire. It was red with neat black handlebars. A girl like her didn't deserve to have such a nice bike. She tried three times to make it to the top of the boulder, panting and sweating, pushing her bike in front of her. Defeated, she hopped on her bike and rode home.

CHAPTER 12

WESTERN MASSACHUSETTS, Berkshire Ridge
May, 1983
Leeann Bright, 12 years old

Helene Bright opened her nursery on the first of May, two weeks later than usual. She didn't explain why but Leeann knew it had to do with her father's leaving. Customers lined up. The saucer magnolias were in full bloom. Tulip-shaped petals lay scattered on the ground. Forsythia bushes draped golden branches over the premises. The ornamental cherry trees had already released pink flowers, and in a week, their leaves would be in full glory. Leeann helped her mother hang baskets of purple petunia at the entrance. She plucked the dead blossoms and watered each basket. She liked the fact that she would be in charge of the nursery for the next hour while her mother ran an errand at the bank.

Leeann turned around to greet the next customers, Mary and Roland Barnes. Mrs. Barnes went to the aisle of clay pots. Mr. Barnes looked at garden hoses.

Leeann closed the cash register drawer and approached Mr. Barnes, who looked up, startled. "Um, when are the police going to find out why your garage burned down?" She gave a thin smile.

Roland took several steps forward and leaned close to Leeann's face. "Why do you want to know that?"

"Just wondered…"

"Stop talking about the fire." He pointed his shaking finger inches from Leeann's face. "You're stirring up trouble."

"I thought…"

"It was a terrible tragedy for the town." In a booming voice, he called to his wife. "Let's go, Mary." Sweat sprang out on his forehead. The edges of his large ears turned red. Towering over Leeann, he shouted, "Stay out of my business."

Leeann took several steps back. Her heart raced. She took a deep breath and looked around the store, hoping to see her mother come through the door. The couple hurried out. Leeann exhaled. She was not going to stop talking to the police or investigators.

As Leeann finished the last spoonful of her ice cream sundae at Mel's Café later that evening, she spotted Traci riding her bike through the parking lot of the railroad station. She hadn't stopped mulling over her confrontation with Roland Barnes, and now, seeing Traci with her freckle-faced smile and choppy, raggedy hair, Leeann put aside her thoughts of that afternoon. Traci's hand shot in the air.

"Why'd you stiff me yesterday? I waited an hour."

"I didn't want to see the fire chief."

Leeann hesitated, not satisfied with the explanation. "You said you'd meet me."

Traci circled Leeann twice and stopped in front of her, screeching her brakes, leaving tire marks. "I hate fire engines and firemen. They remind me of the fire."

"Okay, I won't ask you anymore," Leeann said. Her throat tightened as she watched Traci blink back tears.

They rode until the light faded and clouds filled the sky. At the junction of Windham and Grant, Traci suggested they take the thirty-minute ride around the reservoir.

"It'll be dark soon."

"So?"

"Won't your mom blow a fuse?" Leeann asked.

"No, she doesn't know if I'm home or not."

"If I came home after dark, my mom would turn into dictator-mom Mrs. Mussolini, and I'd be thrown in jail, also known as my room, for a month."

They walked their bikes past Walden Park, nearing the reservoir and dodging cars as they crossed Main Street. They stopped with a lurch when a box truck cut in front of them. As they pushed their bikes along, Leeann tried to talk Traci out of her planned ride. The air was getting colder.

"You could run into a bear or a bobcat. Those woods are spooky."

"I'm not afraid."

"What if you fall off your bike and break your leg and no one hears you yelling?"

"I've done this before." She stopped on the path well before the reservoir's main entrance, now locked for the night. Their walk together ended.

"Well, you'd better take this." Leeann took off her jacket and handed it to Traci, who was wearing a tee-shirt and shorts.

Without saying a word, Traci leapt over the wrought iron fence. She turned and lifted her bike. The ride around the perimeter of the reservoir at that hour seemed plain crazy to Leeann but Traci appeared undaunted. The image of her friend becoming lost or hurt on the edge of all that watery space made Leeann shiver. It was dusk and the trees' muted reflection sketched a thick shadowed ribbon around the water's circumference, leaving the water dark gray on the outside and paler in the middle.

"See you around, Leeann." The wind carried Traci's words. She took off riding, her wheels kicking up dust from the dirt along the jogging path, Leeann's brown jacket melding into the trees. The wind picked up and moved across the reservoir, across its smooth surface, in sudden quick bursts, turning flatness into wrinkles that limped along, quivering, disappearing at the water's edge.

CHAPTER 13

WESTERN MASSACHUSETTS, Berkshire Ridge
June, 1984
Leeann Bright, 13 years old

Leeann's father had been gone over a year. The box of gifts he sent her at Christmas had been his only communication. The box contained a Polaroid camera, Monopoly game, key-chain with a miniature baseball bat dangling from it, and sunglasses. It included no letter and the postmark read, *Sunset District, CA*. Leeann thought of him every day. She knew her mother missed him too, because she continued setting the dinner table for three and left the porch light on every night. Leeann wanted to find her father and bring him home so she could be happy again, so her mother could be happy again. She wished her mother had done more to keep her dad from leaving Berkshire Ridge. She wanted to fly out to California and demand that either he come home or bring the family back together in California.

Two doors down from Mel's Café was McAdam Medical Supply. Every Monday, a van from the Boston store delivered supplies—wheelchairs, bandages, walkers, and canes—to the Berkshire Ridge store, and then the driver, Tim, drove two hours back to Boston. Leeann often started up a conversation with him. This Monday, she offered to help carry supplies into MacAdam's store but Tim declined her offer.

Earlier in the day, her mother had given her permission to have supper and a sleepover at Traci's house. Leeann, instead, climbed into the back of McAdam's van at 3:30 that afternoon, hid behind a hand dolly and several tall boxes, and stowed away to downtown Boston. When McAdam's van reached its destination, Tim lifted the sliding door of the vehicle and left it open while he went into McAdam's store. Leeann leapt onto the street and took off running. She clung to the hope she could find her father in the Sunset District of California. She'd read stories of kids who'd snuck onto airplanes and traveled to faraway cities and knew she could be successful too. The flight to San Francisco was scheduled to leave Logan Airport at 11:00 that evening.

Surrounded by modern buildings and restaurants, Leeann jaunted down Seaport Boulevard, a street wider than any of the others she'd seen a year before during a class trip to the Freedom Trail. The Atlantic was in front of her, and beyond the span of ocean, the airport. A jet plane soared and disappeared behind the clouds. Leeann wondered how to get across the water to her destination. The aroma of pizza drew her into a hole-in-the-wall pizzeria, and she ate two slices and a cup of vanilla ice cream. She resumed her walk on

Seaport Boulevard, stopping once to watch the ocean's swells stirred by a passing fishing boat. The sky appeared as one vast blue canvas, shaded at the horizon by what looked like a dark crayon line of houses in the distance.

A small white car slowed to a crawl and made a U-turn, stopping beside Leeann, pulling within inches of the curb.

The driver opened the passenger window. "Where ya goin'?"

Leeann wondered if the man with the military haircut and square chin was an undercover police officer. Maybe word had gotten out that she'd stowed away inside McAdam's van. She approached the car, smiling, to allay suspicion. But it didn't look like the inside of a police car. Candy wrappers and paper coffee cups were strewn about the front seat.

"The airport," Leeann answered.

"Are you lost?"

"A little."

"Hop in, I'll take you there." The man switched his cigarette to his left hand, leaned across the seat, and opened the passenger door.

Leeann hesitated.

"It's not far," the man said. "You can see the airport from here. There's a plane taking off now." He flashed a grin.

"Well, I don't know…"

"What's your name?"

"Leeann."

"Hey, my sister's name is Leeann." The man adjusted his rear view mirror, then looked back at Leeann. "You look cold standing there. Wind's coming off that ocean. Hurry, get in."

Leeann looked down at her windbreaker and jeans and didn't feel cold.

"I have a sneaky suspicion that you are a lover of the Boston Red Sox." The man pointed to the Red Sox logo on her jacket.

"You're right about that." She rubbed her hand over the logo.

"I bet you play baseball. You're a pitcher, I'd guess."

"I pitch *and* play center field in softball."

"You look athletic. You've got a wicked throwing arm, don't you?"

Leeann tilted her head from side to side. "I guess."

"Remember Ted Williams?" The man put his little finger in his ear and scratched.

"Of course."

"He gave me an official Red Sox bat. Autographed it, too."

Leeann stepped off the curb. She rested her hand on the passenger door. "How'd you get that?"

"Through connections. Want to see it?"

"Yeah." Leeann snuck a peek through the window, hoping to catch sight of the bat.

"It's at my apartment, two blocks from here. Real close." The man leaned over and pushed the passenger door open wider. "Hop in!"

Leeann caught impatience in his voice. But the man would have to wait another minute while she absorbed his clean-shaven face, his grease-slicked hair and his yellow teeth. A medallion hung from the rear view mirror, and the plastic trash bags that filled the back seat nearly blocked the rear window view.

"I'll buy you dinner. Get in." Now his tone was gruff, and he sounded irritated.

Leeann took several steps backward.

"I'm going to walk," she answered. "I don't take rides from strangers."

A sleek red car pulled up behind Leeann, and the white car peeled away, its passenger door still flung open. A middle-aged woman jumped out. "Did you know that man?"

"No," Leeann said, shaking her head.

"Tell me you weren't going to get in that car."

She shook her head again.

"We saw how the creep spun his car around and pulled beside you. But we got his plate number, and I've called the police." The woman looked up and down the street, as if a cruiser was about to appear. "Stay here and you can give a statement to the police."

A younger woman stepped out of the back seat. She swept her long black hair away from her face. Her mouth tightened, but she didn't look as angry as the older woman. "Are you okay? Oh my god." She pressed her hand against her cheek.

Leeann scrambled away from the two women, tripping over her feet. She raced into a parking lot, one so large that she got turned around in the tangle of rows of cars. She emerged from the lot at least a block away from the spot where the strange man had approached her. Her legs were shaking. She leaned over, grasped her thighs, and caught her breath. She waved at a passing taxi, and it screeched to a halt. Ten dollars of birthday money would get her to Logan Airport. She got in the cab. She could trust a taxi driver. He made a sharp turn onto Seaport Boulevard. Leeann scrunched down in her seat but kept her head high enough to view the red car and the two women lingering at the side of the street, speaking to a police officer as the taxi cruised past them.

The night sky was swollen with stars blazing like miniature flames. The Atlantic Ocean was still-black. The break between water and sky was invisible, a blurred boundary in the distance. Leeann observed the scene from the sky-deck at Logan Airport as a 747 soared over Boston Harbor, carrying the reflection of moonlight on its back. Loneliness washed over her. Why hadn't her father called or sent a letter?

"Maybe Dad's in the hospital," she'd said to her mother the week before while sitting at the kitchen table doing homework. "That's why he hasn't called us."

"No, Leeann, your father is working things out." She'd been sitting at the table, too, writing a grocery list.

"He can't talk to us while he's working things out?"

"It has nothing to do with you. Your father's angry at the world."

Leeann didn't buy her explanation. She was certain her father's absence had more to do with her parents' fighting and her father's drinking. Her mother's hand had moved up to cover half of her face, and she'd squeezed her eyes shut, and so, Leeann said nothing. Her mother had gotten up from the table and left her list behind.

Chilly winds pushed her inside and to the waiting lounge and gate from where the flight to San Francisco would leave in four hours. Through square grids of window three stories high, the Boston skyline glinted with skyscrapers, which seemed to rise from the ocean. Leeann maneuvered her way through the crowd of people and found a seat. She smiled when she spotted the couple with three children. She had passed through Security by attaching herself to the youngest child, about four years old. Now, she would blend in with them again and board alongside them.

Leeann waited on the far side of the room, keeping the family of five in close view. She contemplated her plan once in San Francisco. She'd take a cab to the local television station. She'd tell a reporter she was lost and looking for her father. The station would show Leeann's picture on air in San Francisco. She got the idea from a story of a man found circling Boston's Kenmore Square with an LL Bean canvas bag last summer. Within minutes of the station running the story, the man's relatives claimed him. Leeann's father would too. He never missed the TV news.

A view of the black sky and scattered bright lights caused her eyes to fill with tears. She didn't know why. She thought of her mother, who would be in bed, a book in her hands, the radio on. A man appeared from nowhere and asked, "May I see your ticket?"

Leeann fumbled through her pockets. "I lost it." Her heart pounded. She felt the stares of onlookers. Her throat closed.

"Who are you here with?" the officer asked.

"Myself."

"Let's go have a talk."

At Station Five, in the heart of the city, Leeann's story tumbled out. She sat at a desk in a room with two police officers. One wrote down her words as she spoke. Leeann couldn't help thinking that she was sitting in the very chair at times occupied by bank robbers and serial killers. Hands trembling, she asked if she would be going to jail. The officer assured her she would not. He said that a Massachusetts State Trooper would be driving her to Springfield, and an officer from Berkshire Ridge would meet her there and take her home. "But first, let's give your mother a call." Leeann rested her head on her arms. She turned her face to the wall so the officers couldn't see the tears dripping down her cheeks.

In Springfield Leeann climbed into a Berkshire Ridge police cruiser for the ride to her house. She leaned against the door, tilting her head enough to see the driver.

"Hey, I remember you from the talk in my kitchen," Leeann said.

"Yeah, I'm Detective Handley, and I remember you, too." The corners of his mouth turned up. "We meet again."

"My mom's going to have one big holler-fest. I did a bad thing."

Handley told her that he understood how confused she might be feeling. He said his father left the family when he was young, and his mother raised him. "She sacrificed for us. We see these things years later. Be good to your mother, Leeann."

She looked at him through half-closed eyes.

"Appreciate what your mother is doing for you."

"Uh-huh." She yawned, covering her mouth.

"Tell her how sorry you are, and that you'll never leave her again."

"Detective Handley, when are the police going to figure out why the Mechanics Garage burned down?" Her voice was more wide-awake now.

"Why don't you put your head back and get some sleep."

CHAPTER 14

EASTERN MASSACHUSETTS, Boston and surrounding suburbs
1998

A week after Traci announced she was beginning a search for Richard Bright, she and Leeann sat at the bar at Barneys in South Boston, Margaritas in hand.

"I've uncovered some good stuff looking for your dad," Traci said.

"Do you ever consider the hurt you're causing *me*, digging all this up?"

"So I shouldn't clear my father's name because you're uncomfortable with the idea of your dad resurfacing?"

"Finding my father is going to clear your father's name?"

"I have to know." Traci's eyes began to water. "You know, for fifteen years, I've felt like a twelve year old, tugging on adults' sleeves, telling them my dad didn't set the fire at Mechanics Garage. I don't think I can move forward in my life until I find out the truth."

"As I said before, what if you find out he *did* set the fire?"

Traci let out a laugh. "My father did not set the fire."

A sinking, aching sensation grew in Leeann's stomach.

"I've been surfing the Internet and there are a gazillion Richard Brights in San Francisco but I came across an article that made me take notice. It's a review of an art gallery. I want to read it to you." She didn't wait for Leeann's okay.

The newest addition to the Sunset District is a little gem of a gallery featuring the artwork of Canadian-born Richard F. Bright, who specializes in creating paintings of vintage automobiles, antique motorcycles, and classic trucks. His authentic eye and gifted hand make the trip to this unusual shop worthwhile. Open year round; closed Mondays. 47 Seaside Road, Sunset District, CA. Phone:415-387-2222.

"It says he's from Canada. Where was your dad from?"

"Saskatchewan. You know that."

"Right, and he was an auto mechanic. Doesn't it make sense he'd paint cars?"

Leeann picked up her napkin and dabbed her mouth. "No."

"It's possible."

"Unlikely."

"What was your dad's middle name?"

"Frederick."

"On board now?"

"My father was not artistic. Trust me, this is not my father."

"I've got the phone number here. I called the gallery…" Traci took a slow sip of her Margarita. "The phone's been disconnected."

Leeann maintained a blank stare.

"So, I forge ahead." Traci pulled some papers from her pocket. "I was telling my sister about the note Josh got, and she figured out who sent it."

They were seated at the far end of the bar near a live band—it was ballroom dance night at Barney's—where couples crowded onto a shrunken dance floor and swayed to Natalie Cole. Above, a rotating mirror globe cast tiny white spots on their faces and all over their bodies. The spotted, entwined couples danced with flawless steps and pleasant expressions. A burning sensation rose in Leeann's chest.

"Look at that couple out there doing the Foxtrot," Traci said. "Jimmy wanted us to take ballroom dance lessons and I nixed the idea. I'm such a dope." She ran her hand through her hair. "I guess you're not going to ask me about my sister's guess as to the writer of the note."

"Go ahead."

"So, you know Vivian is a hairdresser," she began.

"Yes, continue."

"For years one of Vivian's customers was Mary Barnes, wife of Roland Barnes. Mrs. Barnes has been in a nursing home for several years, and my sister thinks Mrs. Barnes wants to get something off her chest before she dies."

"If she wants to clear her conscience, why didn't she confess it in the note?"

"Maybe what she knows is that Richard Bright knows something," Traci replied. "Anyway, Vivian is going to pay Mrs. Barnes a visit and ask what she knows." The music got louder, and Traci raised her voice. "Do you ever think of him? I mean he is your dad."

Leeann said nothing.

Traci's face softened and she shook her head. "I don't get it. He's alive out there somewhere and…"

"You know what I don't get? A man obsessed with taking his kid canoeing. A man who lights up when he puts his kid on his motorcycle and cruises around Wexler Lake. A man who brings home peppermint Lifesavers for his kid, and makes her guess which hand behind his back is holding them. I can't for the life of me understand how that man can walk away from his kid and never look back."

"So, you're angry."

"Yes, I'm angry. Is that what you want to hear?"

"I want to understand your feelings toward your dad." Traci rubbed the outside of her glass. "I'm no psychologist, but I think men like your father deserted themselves long before they deserted their kids."

Leeann waved her hand at Traci. It was not a good-bye gesture but more of a 'you don't know what the hell you're talking about.'

"A week ago you had no interest and no feelings for him. Now you say you're angry."

"Your point is what?"

"I understand better why you don't want to see him."

"Okay, let's stop analyzing me if you don't mind."

"I'm just saying he left you. I'd be angry too, Leeann."

The band took a break. The sound of instruments was replaced by the hum of voices in the room. Traci asked

Leeann if she wanted to stay at Barneys and have dinner. Leeann declined. She'd had enough of Traci and her research results for one night. They paid their bill and walked to their cars.

After Traci pulled out of the lot and turned toward the highway, Leeann drove to Joanna's Steakhouse on the waterfront. She ate prime rib and popovers. This mess all started with a friggin' anonymous note, she thought. Her life was spinning out of control. Her friendship with Traci was in jeopardy. Her secret could be exposed.

She drank Margarita's and ordered key lime pie. Seated in the center of the room, she was aware of people staring at her, the only woman eating and drinking alone in the noisy, packed, popular restaurant. She was too distraught to care what others thought. At ten o'clock, she stood in front of the Capital Theatre, bought a ticket, and sat down to watch a movie, whose title she couldn't remember after five minutes. The art film, slim on plot about a reformed alcoholic, left her confused. When it was over, she sat alone in the dark. She was wasting her life, bored with her job, although she kept that fact to herself. She wanted to be loved, to have a family. Her friends were getting married and having kids. She wanted a life with joy and didn't know how to go about getting it.

Leeann put down her head. That goddamn Traci, bringing up things she'd tried to forget. And her father. After fifteen years she could hardly picture him, remember his voice or his smell. Any feelings of love for the man were gone, dead, extinct, obliterated. Only anger and resentment lingered. Leeann leaned her elbows on the sides of her chair.

You declared yourself unnecessary to me. We've been apart for fifteen years, and still, it feels like one endless, bewildering day since you backed your truck down the driveway and left. I missed you at dinner, and afterwards, when we used to hang out in the yard or go canoeing or go to Loden's when Mom had her quilting classes. Have you ever thought of us?

A worker in a red vest told her it was time to leave.

CHAPTER 15

EASTERN MASSACHUSETTS, Boston and surrounding suburbs
1998

It wasn't the house that attracted Leeann's attention five years ago when she purchased it, but its gardens, its half-acre of shrubs and perennials. Some might have admired the tall, white pillars, giving the colonial a regal air but Leeann was taken with the seven-foot-high rhododendrons with their full, flat leaves and the rows of astilbe, spine-straight and standing like frozen wintry sticks among the holly bushes. She'd rubbed her hands together, as if squeezing out the night air, while gazing at the lilac bushes, which were scrawny but held promise of recovery. They were bunched together, shrunken and shivering on a hilly embankment, where a white cedar fence met at right angles. She'd envisioned the mud-caked flowerbeds in spring with the early arriving hyacinth pushing through lingering snow and the azalea bushes erupting in grand, white, delicate blossoms.

In those five years, from April through October, Leeann spent hundreds of hours kneeling in the earth, spreading mulch, pulling weeds, trimming leaves, and planting bulbs. She designed drip irrigation systems and created endless serpentine streams of grassy paths twisting around white birches and ornamental cherry trees.

She relished the compliments she received over the years. Strangers rang her doorbell and told her how much pleasure they got from walking past her yard. So, it didn't surprise Leeann to look out her window around five o'clock on Friday afternoon, nine days after her court appearance in Medina, and see a woman bending over her red flowering azalea bushes. The woman twirled around as if to get a better look at the ribbon of multi-colored crocuses stretched across the yard. Her gaze seemed to move to the lilac bushes, not yet in bloom, and to the yellow and purple pansies in one corner.

Leeann had trouble focusing. The glare of the sun cut through her picture window. She couldn't get a good view of the woman's face. It seemed to be the rose bushes, which held the woman's attention. Eight of them formed a boundary on the left side of her yard. Now, they were tiny green buds and were the treasure in her garden. They were her first purchase after she bought the house. Leeann watched the woman lift a leaf on the Medallion rosebush, as though she were handling ancient parchment that might crumble with a touch. When the woman lifted her head, Leeann recognized that orange buzz cut, the sunken cheeks. Holy shit. Karen Downey from Medina. Mother of the biker. Leeann fought the dizziness that overcame her.

Karen Downey approached the front door, and before she could put her finger to the doorbell, Leeann opened it.

"Hello Leeann, Karen Downey here," she said in her dry, husky voice.

Karen offered her hand and they shook. "May we speak?"

Leeann hesitated.

"Just for a moment."

She let her in. Karen stepped over a black sports bag and took the wing chair opposite Leeann on the sofa. Leeann had been nursing a headache all afternoon, and now it was beginning to take on the elements of a migraine. She fought to keep her eyes open. Her elbow throbbed too, a sign of her chronic bursitis.

"You did the right thing pleading guilty in court, and I'd..."

"Hold on a minute, Karen. I pleaded no contest. Big difference." Nervy of her, Leeann thought, finding my house, ringing my doorbell, touching my rosebushes.

"The fallout from Eric's bike accident has resulted in grave consequences for my son and me. Eric now fears going to school. He's in constant pain and is seeing a chiropractor and a neurologist." She folded her hands in her lap. A look of devastation crossed Karen's face, but one so phony that even someone like Leeann, not the most perceptive of people she would admit, could tell it was fake. "He's missing schoolwork and needs a tutor. He has nightmares about the accident, not to mention the loss of his bike. And because he can't help around the house and yard, I've had to hire people. That costs money too." She ran her tongue across her shiny pink lipstick.

Leeann's ears began ringing. Dizziness made the room spin. "You're telling me all this because..."

"My attorney thinks I should sue you in civil court." Here Karen paused ever so slightly, and then, "But I told him I'd settle out of court for five thousand dollars."

"Did you say *five* thousand?"

"Yes, that would put an end to everything."

Leeann wanted to call her a scammer and tell her she was doing damage to Eric by pulling him into her scheme. Instead, her eyes blurred as the migraine set in.

"I know you can't understand this with all the expensive material things you have here, but I'm a single mother trying to make ends meet. I want the best for my son. I need help." She stopped and put her hand to her throat. "May I have some water?"

Leeann wasn't going to tell her she was in too much pain to accommodate her request. She wasn't going to appear weak and incapacitated. She went to the kitchen, swallowed a Vicadin, and returned with a glass of water.

"Karen, you should be contacting my insurance company, shouldn't you?" She sat down again.

"They weren't cooperative. I can't battle a bureaucracy." She covered her forehead and eye with her hand. "I need help," she repeated.

Leeann saw a frailty in Karen. She heard Karen's voice crack and saw her hand shake as she lifted the glass of water to her mouth.

Leeann fought to stay alert. The narcotic she'd taken was making her nauseous. She started to doubt everything about that afternoon in the rain. Maybe her car had skidded on wet pavement, and she had tilted the steering wheel ever so slightly, knocking the boy from his bike. She'd been upset going over Traci's news about the new evidence. She remembered fiddling with the radio. Did she leave the scene and return? Was Eric seriously injured? She wanted Karen out of her house.

"I have cash in the other room. I can give you fifteen hundred dollars and that's all," Leeann said, rubbing her head.

Karen's eyes brightened.

"I can give you that and we can call it a day."

"Very satisfactory." Karen stood up, gripping her purse.

Leeann went to her office, which adjoined the living room. She wondered if Karen heard her opening a file cabinet and rifling through files where she kept an envelope of cash. She counted fifteen hundred dollars in one hundred dollar bills.

"Fifteen hundred dollars must be a drop in the bucket for you. I understand CPA's make oodles of money," Karen said.

Leeann let the comment dissolve in the air and handed her the money in an envelope. "You might want to count it."

And Karen did, while sitting on the edge of a bench in the foyer. She signed the receipt Leeann handed her. "I'm all set," she said, giving a nod in Leeann's direction. She looked over her shoulder. "That chandelier in your dining room must have cost thousands."

"Good luck to you, Karen. My best to Eric." She closed the door behind her. The woman was out of her life. Leeann stumbled back to the sofa. The gruesome episode was behind her. In the midst of her debilitation, she couldn't help but pity Eric Downey, living with a lie to protect his mother.

Hunched over in pain from her head to her elbow, she lay down and stared at the swirls in the ceiling. Her thoughts turned to her own mother, to her mother's green-thumbed self-assuredness, to the elegant movements of her hands and how she liked to place flowers in every room and plants on every surface. She should have been strolling through life right now, in good health and planting bulbs and pruning shrubs and raking leaves. She loved digging up perennials and replanting them in sunnier spots in her yard. Her head for business and her way with customers made for a flourishing nursery and garden shop, the most popular in the region. There should not have been her death at thirty-six or a solemn ceremony of spreading ashes at the Piscataqua River.

Leeann placed a pillow behind her neck and propped up her head. The chill of the room surrounded her. She pulled a blanket over her legs. There should not have been the unrelenting grief that inhabited Leeann for so long.

For two years, the Friday night ritual was the four of them— Traci, Jimmy, Leeann, and Ben—gathering at Leeann's house for the evening. They ordered pizza and barbecue ribs. The beer and Margaritas flowed. Ben and Jimmy talked about sports or computers for hours. Sometimes a movie occupied the four of them. On other nights, Leeann and Traci watched a mystery movie on TV or talked about where their next trip together might take them—skiing in Vermont, four days in Bermuda or maybe a weeklong trip to London. The ritual ended after Leeann's break-up with Ben. And so, when Traci called on Friday to ask if she could stay at her house for a few days, Leeann was happy for the company.

Traci walked into Leeann's house after work announcing, "Guess who died?" She turned her mouth in to an exagerrated frown. "Mary Barnes. I told my sister a week ago that Mrs. Barnes is not going to live forever and she'd better get down to that nursing home. But she was too busy planning her neighbor's friggin' baby shower."

"Listen, Traci, Mary Barnes did not write the anonymous note," Leeann insisted. "That handwriting is masculine."

"How do you know?"

"I'm a CPA. I watch men and women sign corporate tax returns every day. I know the difference between male and female handwriting," Leeann insisted.

"This handwriting belonged to Mary Barnes. I'm positive she knew something." Traci shook her head. "Damn stinking bad luck of mine."

"No, sorry, this handwriting belongs to a man."

Traci pointed to Leeann's arm. "What's up with the sling?"

"My bursitis is acting up. No tennis for a while."

Traci whipped around Leeann's kitchen preparing cheeseburgers and baked potatoes. Leeann tried opening a bottle of Merlot with one hand but couldn't. Traci took over and pulled the cork out of the bottle.

"But, I do have good news," Traci said, standing at the stove.

Leeann didn't like the overly cheerful tone Traci used. She didn't like the way Traci's eyebrows shot up in an exaggerated way when she said, 'good news.' She braced herself and poured the wine.

"Well, first of all, I had dinner with my Uncle Ray last week. He's the one who coaches hockey at Massachusetts University. Remember?"

"The one you had a grudge against for years?" Leeann asked.

"My parents did. When my mom died, my sisters and I reconnected with him."

Leeann figured the real 'good news' had little to do with Uncle Ray.

"Anyway, our dinner was fortuitous." She put both arms out to her side, palms upward. "He was leaving for San Francisco the next day on business."

When Leeann heard 'San Francisco,' she tipped her head back and groaned.

"I asked him if I could pay him to take a detour drive to the Sunset District and check out Richard Bright's Art Gallery."

"Why do you keep pushing this on me?" Leeann's jaw tightened. "This is your mission, and I commend you for it but I don't want to hear anything about my father, lost or found."

Traci continued. "When I told Uncle Ray the reason for the favor, of course he said yes."

"Of course."

"I'm picking him up tomorrow afternoon at Logan and hearing about his reconnaisance. We're going out afterwards to Tony's-on-the-Waterfront in the Seaport District. Come with us." Leeann stared at her and said nothing. "You'll find Ray fascinating. He has lots of stories about the Bruins. He knows all the players."

"Really? Any of them single?" Leeann flashed a pretend-smile.

Traci responded with the same pretend-smile. She stood up and cleared her plate from the table. "If it wasn't Mary Barnes, then who wrote the note?"

"Someone who had it in for my dad, maybe. Or, one of the firemen who was at the scene that night and wants to start trouble."

"Fifteen years later?"

Leeann picked at the food getting cold on her plate.

CHAPTER 16

EASTERN MASSACHUSETTS, Boston and surrounding suburbs
1998

"I had no trouble finding my way down the coast to the Sunset District," Ray began. "Gorgeous scenery." He faced Leeann and Traci in the baggage claim area at Logan Airport. He and Leeann chatted for a few minutes about his flight. He asked why her arm was in a sling, and she explained it was bursitis. Traci interrupted with, "Okay, okay, enough chitchat. Let's sit down and hear about Ray's trip." She pointed to some empty chairs.

"I found some fascinating stuff." He looked at Leeann and then at Traci.

Traci moved closer to him, turning her back to Leeann. Leeann leaned forward, trying to shut out the litany of loudspeaker announcements.

"Once I got to the center of town, somebody told me that Richard Bright's gallery was on Seaside Road, a little side street, which, it turned out, was real close to the Pacific Ocean." Traci nodded. "So, now I'm on Seaside Road, and I look up and see this purple and gold sign hanging over a shop door in the distance, and as I got closer, I saw that it read, 'Richard Bright Gallery.' Leeann began to sweat. "So I'm thinking this is *way* too easy. There it is. In two minutes I'll be inside that store, talking to the artist, and finding out if he's part of the Bright clan from Canada and Berkshire Ridge, Massachusetts. I could be talking to Leeann's dad." He said this looking straight at Leeann and then paused. Traci's hand made a rolling motion, as if to say to him, 'keep going, keep going.' "So when I get to the front door, I see the whole place is locked up. It was eleven o'clock in the morning. And then I see a sign on the door that read, 'closed indefinitely for renovations.' "

Traci put her hands over her face. "God, no."

"The store front window was covered in newspaper," he continued. "I couldn't see anything inside, just blackness in between gaps of newspaper. So, I went to the shop next door, a jewelry store, and asked the clerk, a woman about my age, if she knew Richard Bright. Her face lit up like a strobe light. 'I've met him a few times,' she said. Her name was Astrid Bloom." Traci's forehead was a streak of deep-in-thought wrinkles. "So I told her I was this huge fan of Richard's and asked if she knew how I might reach him. She said he moved his gallery into one side of Tang's Frame Shop a year ago, and then recently an electrical fire caused damage to both stores. Carpenters told her that the place would be re-opening in several weeks." He looked at Traci. "So I ended up buying a moonstone necklace for your Aunt Jean just to keep the woman talking."

Traci took a deep breath and exhaled. "This is quite the story."

Ray went on. "I asked her what Richard was like and she said 'a quiet man.' "

A growing swarm of people filled the baggage claim area. Ray raised his voice over the chatter. When the carousel started to move, a teenage boy wheeled his suitcase over Leeann's loafered-toes and kept on walking. A woman's shoulder bag swung within an inch of Ray's face. Ray put up his hand as if to block a near-hit and kept talking. "Astrid Bloom said he was in his sixties with bushy red hair and a reddish beard."

"Your dad had red hair like you," Traci said, turning to Leeann and sitting up straight in her chair.

Ray continued, "She said she didn't know where Richard lives or where I could write to him other than to the store. I told her I'd be coming back to San Francisco in a few months. We exchanged business cards and she told me to call her before I come and she'd let me know if the store is open and if Richard is around. And then I left."

Traci's shoulders went limp. "So we don't know much."

"We don't know anything," Leeann added. "Can we go to dinner now? I'm starving." She thought about the veal parmigiana and canoli she'd be ordering at Tony's-on-the-Waterfront.

"Wait, there's much more but I've got to grab my suitcase." Ray hurried toward the carousel. Leeann and Traci said nothing to one another. When he returned, Traci said, "So let's hear what else you have."

Ray reached into his suitcase and pulled out a folded-up, yellow piece of paper. "I went back to Richard's store and copied down this newspaper article, which had been framed and hung in the store window."

Leeann fixed her eyes squarely on Ray's lips. Slowly and loudly, he read:

Paintings of vintage trucks, classic cars, and antique motorcycles fill the newest gallery on Seaside Road's retail strip. And the artist behind the amazing creations in the one-room gallery with low ceilings and glistening floors is Richard 'Rod' Bright.

"People called your dad Rod, didn't they?" Traci asked. Leeann shrugged.

Bright's works are a celebration of a culture that lives for and loves its automobiles. His buoyant canvases bring alive memories of yesteryear: first date in a 1947 Buick; prom night driving a 1952 Ford Mustang; first purchase of a 1960 Chrysler as a newly married couple; riding in grandpa's 1933 Buick; pulling into a gas station and parking beside a 1938 Pontiac. His paintings reveal a true craftsman with an eye for precision, a hand for detail, and a passion for his subject matter. Yet, Bright, originally from Saskatchewan, Canada, didn't begin his painting life until he reached his mid-forties. Hospitalized with a broken leg from a construction accident and hung up in a cast for weeks, a friend brought him paints and brushes to help pass time. Not knowing what to start painting, he thought of the cars and trucks he used to fix as a mechanic back in Western Massachusetts.

A chill rolled through Leeann's body.

As he turned out one painting after another, people marveled at his talent. For the next ten years he painted only for pleasure before establishing a gallery and selling his works. Visit the Richard Bright Gallery and view his impressive paintings, which conjure up a love of bygone decades, when life was simple and people really did look at the world through polished, optimistic, rose-colored windshields.

"So what do you think?" he asked, almost breathless.

"It's him," Traci said. "The Western Massachusetts connection, the red hair, the nickname, the career as a mechanic. I knew it."

"Doubtful," Leeann said.

Traci threw up her hands. "If you don't think this man is your father, you're delusional."

Standing now, Leeann looked for exit signs. It was after six o'clock and getting dark. She wanted to go home, warm up some leftover meatloaf, watch *Friends* on TV, and go to bed. But she was stuck with Ray and Traci for the evening. She let out a groan so loud that the woman in front of her turned around and stared. The three of them made their way to the parking garage. Ray offered to drive them to the restaurant, not far from the airport. Leeann stretched out in the back seat of Ray's SUV but not before she saw Ray and Traci exchange glances, as if they'd been talking about her, and that unnerved her. She cradled her injured arm and rubbed her hand along the rough-textured fabric of her sling. They drove without speaking until Traci broke the silence.

"Doing okay back there, Leeann?"

"Never been better," she snapped.

"Looks as if I'll be going to San Francisco." Traci hesitated. "Will you come with me, Leeann?"

She chose to let the question go unanswered, and Traci didn't ask again. Leeann stared out the window and tried to block Richard Bright from her mind. She took in the hugeness of the sky, the ceiling of stars, the oily black Atlantic, running parallel to the road. A motorboat passed them and the ocean erupted with ferocious swells. Leeann couldn't stop thinking that some sort of major trouble lay ahead.

CHAPTER 17

EASTERN MASSACHUSETTS, Boston and surrounding suburbs
1998

On Sunday morning, Traci pushed a plate of French toast across the table toward Leeann.

"When are you heading home?" Leeann asked.

"Trying to get rid of me?"

"Course not. Tomorrow's Monday. I thought you'd need to go home and get ready for the week."

"I've got nothing waiting for me there. I was hoping you'd let me stay awhile." She picked up a napkin and wiped maple syrup off her face.

"You don't even have to ask."

"Think about what you want me to help you with today," she said, getting up. "If I'm going to crash here, I should at least be useful."

"You don't have to be useful."

They moved to the living room and sat down with their coffee. For the next hour they read the Sunday newspaper.

Leeann thought about the news from Ray the day before, and the possibility that the artist Richard Bright could be her father. What was she worried about? If Richard Bright the artist, turned out to be her father, he would never admit to Traci he had anything to do with the fire. He'd appear confused and deny he knew anything. He'd look at Traci as if she were crazy. No, she had nothing to worry about. Traci might go to San Francisco, might even sit with Richard Bright face to face, but she'd come home empty handed.

Later that afternoon, Traci stood at Leeann's living room window. "A man's outside looking at your garden."

"Some days it's like a parade out there. People love looking at my yard."

"Wait, he's coming up your front walk." Traci answered the door to a middle-aged man with thick hair and two large moles on his cheek.

"You Leeann Bright?"

"She's over there." Traci pointed to Leeann, who muted the TV and tripped over the coffee table leg before reaching the man's side.

"Constable Sanderson. I'm serving you with these documents."

"From whom?"

"It's in the envelope." The man turned and left but not before giving a spot-check to the Chinese vase on the fireplace mantle, to the chandelier in the distance, to the newspapers on the floor.

Leeann pulled the papers from the envelope. "Holy shit."

"What?"

"It's a lawsuit from Karen Downey. She's suing me for two hundred fifty thousand dollars. She wants me to pay for damages to her and her son resulting from the bike accident I allegedly caused." The papers slipped from Leeann's hand, and she left them on the floor.

"I told you she's a certified nutcase."

"This is serious, Traci. She's out to take away everything I have." She sunk in to the sofa. "I wasn't going to tell you this but the flimflam artist showed up at my house Friday afternoon. I'd called in sick because I wanted a day to myself and ended up getting a migraine and flare-up of my bursitis. Leeann closed her eyes. "I gave her money."

Traci's eyes widened. "How much?"

"Fifteen hundred."

"Have you gone mad?" She jumped off the chair and flung out her arms. "Why would a smart woman who's in the finance field, no less, do something so stupid?"

"She said a few hundred bucks would make her go away. She even signed a receipt. She's evil."

Traci continued chastising her for such a 'totally dumb move.'

"I wanted nothing more to do with courts and police and attorneys, and I thought money would make her go away for good."

"Still doesn't make sense why such an intelligent…"

"Stop making me feel worse than I already do." They sat in the living room, looking at one another, shaking their heads, passing the legal papers back and forth.

"There's no attorney listed in these documents."

"She's representing herself," Leeann said.

"Can she do that?"

"Anyone can walk into court and file a lawsuit." Leeann grabbed Traci's arm. "Listen, do *not* tell Ben I gave money to Karen Downey. You think I don't feel like a moron? Karen Downey seemed so pathetically sympathetic. I had a migraine. I was drugged and in pain and out of my mind."

CHAPTER 18

WESTERN MASSACHUSETTS, Berkshire Ridge
July, 1984
Leeann Bright, 13 years old

Helene Bright's customers at the Blue Iris Nursery typically chose variegated ivy or pothos or another hardy, leafy, green plant to put in a corner on a table in the path of the sun. But in Leeann's zeal, manning the indoor plant counter that Saturday morning, she tried talking an elderly man into purchasing a pink Vanda orchid or a show-quality African violet. The man tried to decline any high-maintenance species, but Leeann sent him home with a sensitive tropical begonia, free of charge, and told him he'd find out it was a cool, colorful plant.

"Most people don't want to sweat over their plants, Leeann. Let them have their easy-to-maintain pothos." Helene Bright leaned into her daughter and narrowed her eyes. "And stop giving away the plants."

Leeann didn't argue. She removed her gardening gloves and wiped her forehead with the back of her hand before emptying the register. She put out her hand to her mother to collect the money she'd earned that week, already planning to spend it at the Berkshire Ridge State Fair with Traci that afternoon.

Leeann met Traci at Mel's Cafe, and they rode their bikes for a half hour to the State Fair off Highway Nineteen north of Vernon. Chloe's Famous Hot Dog Stand was known for its foot-long hotdogs and skinny French fries, drenched in salt. Leeann decided it would be her first stop at the fair.

It was a steaming day in July. Beyond the entrance gate were crowds of people of all ages. Leeann became giddy at the roar of the roller coaster and piped-in ragtime music. The aroma of sausages and onions wafted her way. Most people were eating something—cotton candy, corndogs or ice cream cones. Many held prizes in their arms—large stuffed bears, pandas, and even a stuffed octopus. There were slap-happy smiles on all the kids' faces.

Traci demanded they ride the Ferris-wheel. While Leeann bought her ticket, Traci chatted with the ride operator. She must have said something hilarious because the man let out a deep belly laugh and patted Traci on the head. In seconds, they left the ground behind and were high above the fair, taking in a view of the rides, the petting zoo, the pond, and hundreds of people meandering through the fairgrounds. Both tipped their faces toward the sun.

When they reached the top for the second time, the wheel stopped, and their seat rocked back and forth. Leeann let out an exaggerated shriek. Traci moved her body from side to side until the seat swung so precariously that Leeann, laughing, begged her to stop. The two girls looked at one another and grinned, Leeann thinking this was one of the best days in her life.

When the ride ended, the operator helped everyone out of their seats but didn't release the metal safety bar for Traci and Leeann. He checked that it was secure and let them ride again for free three more times.

By the end of the afternoon, they'd ridden the Bumper Cars five times and the Whip eight. They'd bounced up and down on the Caterpillar and lost their breaths on the Tilt-a-Wheel. They'd rented paddleboats and circled the manmade pond next to the grassy park and picnic tables. They'd eaten so much cotton candy they agreed they might throw up. After taking several rides on two old thoroughbreds, it was time to leave in order for Leeann to make her six o'clock curfew.

"If I'm five minutes late, my mom turns into a scream machine."

Traci insisted they take one last ride on the Ferris wheel.

Leeann reached into her jeans pocket. "I'm out of money."

"I'll treat."

They climbed in and bounced up and down in their seat but settled down after the ride took off. At the top of the wheel, Leeann couldn't believe how much space the fairgrounds inhabited and how far into the distance she could see. "We haven't moved in five minutes," she soon complained.

"What do you think is wrong?" Traci asked, her voice cracking.

Leeann's hands flapped in the air. "Get us down!" She realized from the parade of firefighters, TV news crews and paramedics below that the ride had broken down. A man with a bullhorn announced that the Ferris wheel had indeed malfunctioned. "Stay calm, we'll have you down shortly."

"Is your mom going to be mad?" Traci asked.

"Yes." But Leeann forgot about missing curfew when Traci began talking about the rides they'd been on and the food they'd eaten. They talked about their teachers and the school's football team—which boys were the cutest—and about school. They were pumped about being assigned to Mrs. Taylor's homeroom and not Mr. Renkel's. The late afternoon wind blew through the grounds and pushed their seat into motion every few minutes. And when it did, both girls grabbed onto one another and put on a frightened face that was more real than pretend. They played the cloud game.

Traci pointed. "I see an old man with a beard in that cloud."

"I see a bird with wings stretched out."

"I see a rabbit."

"You're making that up." The cloud game preoccupied them until Leeann tapped Traci on the shoulder and said she had a joke for her. "What kind of music did the pilgrims play?"

Traci shrugged.

"Plymouth rock."

Traci laughed for a half-second, and the Ferris wheel began moving. It had taken thirty minutes. Both girls declined to be interviewed by Channel 5 though the TV news cameras were rolling when the operator helped them out of their seats, and when Traci gave a victory signal with her two clasped hands in the air. By six, they were back on their bikes and on Highway Nineteen.

After leaving Traci at Mel's Cafe, Leeann continued biking home and noticed a car following her. She was sure it was the same car that had been following the two of them for several blocks. She peddled faster than she'd ever peddled before yet the car stayed on her trail. To shorten her ride home, she cut through the alley that ran behind the shops on Myrtle Street. The light in the sky was fading. Dullness fell over the empty streets. Shadows darkened lawns. She'd missed curfew an hour ago. The car followed her into the alley. She continued on her bike, though more slowly, and the car slowed down too, close behind her almost bumper to bumper. Leeann stopped to let the car pass, but it stopped as well. It had its lights on, and the two bright beams lit up her bike. Leeann got back on her bike, and the car began moving. She tried to swerve around a cinder block lying in her way, but her wheel caught it and she and the bike went down, her head barely missing a broken beer bottle. Leeann lay there. The car braked sharply to a stop. A man got out of the driver's side.

"Mr. Barnes, it's you, hi," she said, getting to her feet. She pulled gravel out of her hair. The side of her face felt wet and burning. "Sorry I was in your way."

Roland Barnes charged at Leeann, grabbed her shoulders, and slammed her against the brick wall of AJ's Auto Body Shop. Leeann felt the man's biceps bearing down on her. The back of her head hit the brick surface hard.

"It seems you can't keep your mouth shut."

"I'm sorry."

"For months, you've been going around asking the police and fire department what happened at my place. What the hell for?" Moisture oozed above Roland's fleshy lips. He smelled of alcohol, and his eyes took the form of two black circles. He pushed Leeann's body against the wall again.

"It's my friend, Traci Stylofski. Everyone's blaming her dad."

"Yeah, Norm Stylofski." Roland blinked hard. "What happened at my place is none of your business. You understand?" He still had a grip on Leeann's shoulders. Leeann managed a nod. "You're stirring up trouble." He enunciated each syllable, spitting into Leeann's face "No one wants to think about the fire anymore." A purple vein sprouted on his forehead. "Keep your mouth shut."

Leeann didn't dare move.

Roland towered over her. "You don't want anything to happen to the little bit of family you have left, do you? Your mom? Or your mom's nursery?"

It took Leeann a minute to absorb Roland's threats. She shook her head.

Roland gave her a parting shove. Leeann warbled on her feet, holding onto the side of the building. She watched Roland get into his Lincoln Town Car and back down the alley.

Leeann's legs were still trembling when she reached her house two blocks away. She threw her bike onto the ground and raced up the back stairs. The kitchen was dark. She thought her mother must be in the living room, waiting. Her anger over Leeann missing curfew would spill out slowly at first, a quiet restraint of words, and then become a full-blown holler fest. But in the living room, a man was sitting in front of the television. He stood up and turned to Leeann. It was John Wicker, a heavy, bearded man in his forties, and the assistant manager at the nursery. When Helene Bright began her business, neighbors and shop owners told her she couldn't find a better person to help run her nursery than John Wicker. He'd been a landscaper in town and now worked the same long hours that her mother did as though he was the owner of the four acres.

"Where's my mom?" Leeann asked, looking around the room.

"Your mom's at Berkshire Hospital. She collapsed outside the garden shop."

"The hospital!"

"Hey, what happened to your face?"

"I've got to go see my mom right now." Leeann's words were a rapid fire of panic. Roland had hurt her mother.

"Don't worry, doctors said it was dehydration and high blood pressure."

"I've got to see my mom. Someone hurt her. She might have been poisoned." Leeann covered her face with her hands.

"No, no, she's going to be fine."

"If you won't drive me to the hospital, I'll ride my bike. I've got to see my mom." She continued to hold her head in her hands, as though her brain pulsed with pain. "My mom was poisoned," she repeated.

"Where are you getting these thoughts?"

"Please take me there." She was shaking, and her head was throbbing.

John reminded Leeann that visiting hours were over and got Leeann to sit down and take deep breaths. He said they could call her mother, and she could hear for herself that she was okay. And then they should wash her face and put a bandage on her cut. Leeann nodded.

Helene Bright sounded fine on the phone, at first a little drowsy from having been woken. She must have heard the urgency in Leeann's voice because she assured her daughter that all the tests confirmed she was in good shape.

"We got stuck on the Ferris wheel. At the very top. You'll see it in the paper tomorrow, and I might be on TV tonight." It was Leeann's turn to reassure her mother that she and Traci had stayed calm.

"I know you were brave. Listen, John's going to keep you company tonight."

"I don't need a babysitter, Mom. I'm thirteen." Leeann paused. She remembered how two weeks before, she and her mother had stayed up talking on the night Detective Handley brought her home from Logan Airport, and how she'd apologized to her mother and promised she would stop being so oppositional—her mother's word. "But it's okay, I like John."

"That's good, Leeann. I'm sorry I'm here. I have so much to do—bills, the laundry, shopping, the nursery payroll." In a hoarse, sleepy voice, her mother told her she would see her in the morning. Before hanging up, she told her daughter not to worry so much.

Upstairs, in the bathroom, John's large fingers dabbed a cotton ball on Leeann's face to wash off the dried blood and dirt. With another cotton ball, he applied hydrogen peroxide to her wound.

"I'll make you dinner," he said.

"I ate enough today."

"You sure everything's okay?"

"Everything's okay." She watched John turn and go downstairs. The television went back on. There were loud voices and laughter. Exhausted, Leeann climbed into bed and pulled the covers over her.

Don't worry? How could her mother have said that? There were so many things to worry about, so many things she couldn't tell her mother. It wasn't like before. Now there were secrets and problems she had to figure out on her own. She had troubles, adult-size troubles. They crowded out the things she used to think about: softball, bike riding, working on her ship models and painting her lead figures. Some days she had no interest in doing any of the things she loved before the Mechanics Garage fire. Now, she moped around the house after school and couldn't concentrate on her homework. She tossed and turned, trying to wipe away the image of Roland Barnes standing over her, raging and threatening, looking like a monster that rivaled anything she'd seen in the movies.

CHAPTER 19

WESTERN MASSACHUSETTS, Berkshire Ridge
September, 1984
Leeann Bright, 13 years old

For the fifth time in the first month of school, Leeann went to see the nurse, Ms. Tucker, with complaints of stomach pain. She walked in hunched over, clutching her stomach.

"You're back?" Ms. Tucker was a tall, slim woman in her mid-twenties. The nurse's office was a windowless room with a metal desk near the door and a cot in the corner. The room smelled of rubbing alcohol and iodine.

"Another stomachache," Leeann groaned.

Ms. Tucker raised her eyebrows, her blue eyes shining through petite glasses. "Something is certainly troubling you, or I should say, your stomach."

As if on cue, a wave of tightness pulled at Leeann's insides.

"Did you eat a lot of candy or ice cream last night?"

Leeann rattled off her meals, and they were healthy meals, not like those Traci ate—potato chips for breakfast, apple pie for dinner. She answered the nurse's questions. No, she wasn't nauseous. Yes, the pain began after she arrived at school that morning.

"We'll fix you right up like we always do," she said. Some of Leeann's friends thought it was funny Ms. Tucker referred to herself as "we," as in "we'll put a bandage on that cut of yours," or "we'll take a good look at your sore throat."

Leeann didn't mind the 'we.' She would have been happy to have a stomachache every day just so she could visit Ms. Tucker, and she didn't care what Ms. Tucker called herself.

"Let me feel your hands." She took them in her own and rubbed them together. "So cold." She guided Leeann to the orange plastic chair next to her desk. Leeann continued holding her stomach, the acidic burn rising from deep in her gut to her esophagus. Her eyes could barely focus on the long blue beads Ms. Tucker wore around her neck. They rested against her ample breasts. She put a thermometer into Leeann's mouth. "Your temp is normal." She investigated the location of Leeann's pain, gently pressing on her stomach. Leeann shivered at the sensation of the cold stethoscope on her back and chest. Ms. Tucker examined her eyes, ears, and throat, her face never changing from its reassuring smile. Ms. Tucker had Leeann sit beside her and slowly sip a glass of warm water.

"You're doing fine."

The water felt good going into Leeann's mouth, and when she was through drinking, she lay on the cot. Ms. Tucker placed a wool blanket over her. It felt itchy, but Leeann didn't complain. She closed her eyes, opening them every so often to peek at Ms. Tucker sitting at her desk. Her head was tilted down, as though she was reading something. A crystal-studded barrette secured the blond curls piled on top of her head.

"Ms. Tucker, have you ever told a lie?" Leeann raised her head off the cot.

"Why yes, I suppose I have." She toyed with her pearl earring. "Are you asking because you've told a lie, Leeann?"

She nodded.

"Big or small?" Her voice was playful.

"Big."

"Whom did you lie to?" Now, her tone grew serious.

"My mom."

"I think you should tell your mom the truth." Her earring dropped onto the desk. It rolled around on the metal surface before falling onto the floor. She leaned down and picked it up. "It doesn't have to be today or tomorrow, but when you feel ready, you should confide in her." She struggled to put her earring into the tiny hole in her earlobe.

Leeann lay down and closed her eyes.

"Do you want to tell me what the lie is about, Leeann?"

She shook her head.

"But it's bothering you, isn't it?"

"Yeah."

"Well, everyone lies at some time. It's not a good idea to do often." She pulled her barrette from her hair and repositioned it on top of a sweep of hair. "You'll be glad once you tell your mom the truth."

Surrounding Leeann were white walls and white cabinets. The floor was mostly white with an occasional black tile. Even Ms. Tucker's uniform was white, and something about all that white gave Leeann the feeling she was in competent hands. After thirty minutes, she told Ms. Tucker that her stomachache was gone and that she was ready to go back to class. She began to saunter out of the office.

"Wait, Leeann," Ms. Tucker called out. She put aside her pen and manila folder. "I'm going to advise your mom to take you to your family physician."

"For a stomachache?"

"Your stomachaches are becoming frequent."

Leeann made a face.

Ms. Tucker untangled the blue beads knotted in the stethoscope. "I'm sure it's nothing serious."

On the day of the doctor's appointment, Leeann claimed she felt sick and spent the morning on the sofa in front of the TV watching old westerns. Her mother rushed through the door at noon. She was sweaty and smelled like cedar mulch. She'd been working on a landscaping job at the library. After a check on Leeann's condition, she took a shower, put on a pink blouse and green slacks, and tied her hair in a ponytail. She smeared her lips with raspberry colored lipstick. She was all business. "Leeann, wear your slacks, not shorts, and don't dawdle."

Leeann rolled off the sofa as her mother carried on.

"And why didn't you put the butter back in the refrigerator? Look," she barked and pointed to the floor. "The ants will be all over those crumbs you dropped, and I found muddy footprints in the hallway that you need to clean up." It wasn't unusual for her mother, under stress, to get mad and order her around. To her friends, Leeann sometimes called her 'my mom, the drill sergeant.'

The doctor's office was in downtown Berkshire Ridge in a three-story faded brick building. They parked in the newly paved lot beside an expanse of lawn. A pine tree at the edge of the lot lifted its branches and made moving shadows across the lawn. A chipmunk raced across the grass and ducked under a low-lying pine branch.

They paused at the front door while Leeann's mother stared at the flowerbed. It held three scraggly domed bushes, wilted from the summer heat. Leeann knew what her mother was thinking: No colorful flowers beneath the bushes to honor the natural world? No purple salvia, no pink phlox, no white petunias? She was always saying that flowers were as magnificent as if they were colors on canvas. "No one could find time to stick a handful of geraniums in the ground? They'd need hardly any care," she said, as she opened the door.

Leeann was looking forward to seeing Dr. Douglas Turtle. His bookshelves were filled with replicas of turtles in all sizes and textures—plastic, wooden, clay, stone, rubber, and cloth. If you had to go to a pediatrician, kids in town agreed the coolest place to go was Dr. Turtle's office. Each child picked a favorite turtle and held it, while the doctor performed his examination. Leeann figured that the little kids liked the soft stuffed ones, but she picked up a wooden turtle and put it beside her after turning it over several times in her hand and studying the markings on its shell. Dr. Turtle was one of the oldest pediatricians in Berkshire Ridge. His skin was slightly gray, his hair the color and texture of straw.

Dr. Turtle examined her just as Ms. Tucker had. Leeann focused her attention on the wispy hair growing from his ears. When he was done, he asked Leeann a question Ms. Tucker never asked. "Have you been sad or worried lately?"

Leeann was so flustered by the question that she answered without stopping to think. "No."

"I assure you, Leeann's been doing exceptionally well, given what's been going on in our family."

"Don't sound so offended, Mrs. Bright. It's a necessary question."

"I'm not offended, just…I don't know, surprised, maybe."

Dr. Turtle's eyes shifted from Leeann to her mother and back to Leeann. "I'd like to talk to your mother alone, Leeann. Would you mind waiting in the other room?"

Leeann bounced from the examining table, intent on finishing the National Geographic article about Iceland. But worries took hold as she waited, wondering if she was deathly sick or had a rare stomach disease.

And when she returned to the doctor's office, it was the calm expression on her mother's face that brought her relief.

"I'm prescribing medication for your stomachaches," Dr. Turtle explained, handing Leeann an orange bottle with thirty pills inside. "Take one pill at the onset of pain or discomfort." He patted his own stomach as he explained. "The pill will melt under your tongue, and the pain will go away."

Leeann jumped down off the examining table. "I don't mind taking pills. I'm just glad I didn't have to get a shot in my arm or somewhere else."

"You're going to be fine," he said. "And when you need refills, you stop by my office. I'll give them to you for free."

Leeann's mother thanked the doctor. She said she'd let him know how the treatment was working.

"Mrs. Bright, you are taking care of *yourself*, aren't you? You're not working too hard?" Dr. Turtle asked. He held the door open for Leeann and her mother.

"I'm running a business and raising a thirteen year old." She lifted her shoulders and let them drop. "Not much time for rest." In the elevator, she remarked to Leeann, "He's a wonderful doctor."

Leeann and her mother ordered ice cream sodas at Mel's Café across the street from the medical building. Sitting by the picture window, Leeann wolfed down her soda. Her mother ate slowly, stopping now and then to announce the names of individuals who were entering and exiting the medical building. "There goes Libby Wilson with Josh. Poor boy has leukemia. Don't spread that around, Leeann. It's supposed to be hush-hush." Leeann nodded. "Josh is one year behind you in school?"

Leeann picked up a napkin and wiped ice cream off her face. "No, same class."

"That family has been through hell."

It was Leeann who pointed out that Dr. Turtle was coming out of the building carrying a briefcase and folders in his arm. In front of the flowerbed, he dropped the folders and struggled to gather them up. Leeann and her mother watched the doctor clumsily get into the driver's side of his black Cadillac. Leeann couldn't help thinking it must be awful to get old. Dr. Turtle's car moved forward, then backward, then lurched forward again over a low cement barrier. The car engine roared, but the car, trapped, didn't move. Leeann's mother shouted, "Run across the street and tell the doctor I'll have Mel call him a tow truck."

Dr. Turtle was shaken up. His glasses were lying on the passenger seat. His head must have hit the steering wheel because he was rubbing his forehead. His fingers moved in a circular motion on his temples. Leeann opened the car door. "You okay, Dr. Turtle?"

Although the doctor replied that he was fine, he looked dazed and unfocused. Leeann stayed at his side, patting his shoulder, until Cecil's Tow Service arrived.

CHAPTER 20

WESTERN MASSACHUSETTS, Berkshire Ridge
October, 1984
Leeann Bright, 13 years old

It was the end of October, and Western Massachusetts was deep into autumn. The foliage proved to be cheerless. The maples produced washed out shades of color, tinting the landscape with an eerie dullness. The yellows looked more like drab butterscotch than lemony-gold. The reds had a pervasive brown haze. And when leaves became brittle, they fell from the trees and formed piles of rusty brown litter that tarnished sidewalks and clogged sewers.

Leeann faithfully carried her pills in her pocket to school and the nursery and the softball field. If pain occurred at school, she would ask her teacher for permission to go to the bathroom, and in the stall, slip a pill under her tongue and wait for it to dissolve. Within a few minutes, she would feel fine.

Most of her stomach discomfort occurred at school, but on this day, the last Friday in October at the nursery, she recognized the familiar gnawing inside her gut. She headed to the shed behind the green house to take a pill. She started to enter, then hesitated. There were voices inside. Her fingers let go of the rusty latch. She ran her hand across the prickly surface of the shed's unfinished wood wall and put her head against the door to hear faint murmuring and a muffled giggle. Leeann pushed the door open. In front of her stood her mother and John Wicker, an arm around a shoulder, another arm around a waist. Body against body. Head against head. Lip against lip. The two spun around to meet Leeann's open-mouth stare. Her mother too, opened her mouth as if to utter something, but no words came out. Leeann clenched her teeth until she heard grinding sounds, and a searing pain traveled through her jaw. She turned, red-faced, and ran to the garden shop, where she could lose herself among customers, who wanted to know how to plant tulip bulbs before the ground froze.

Before dinner, her mother knocked on Leeann's bedroom door. "Okay to come in?"

"Ahh, okay."

Her mother sat on the edge of Leeann's bed. Her hand ran across the blue quilted spread she'd made in quilting class that spring.

"I'm *very* sorry about what happened this afternoon."

"Okay." Leeann avoided looking at her mother's face.

"John asked me to go out with him, and I reminded him I was still married."

"Mom, I've got homework," Leeann said, even though Seventeen Magazine lay on her lap. She picked up her geometry book.

"Yes, John did kiss me. Yes, that was inappropriate. I should not have let it happen." Her mother sat there for another minute, playing with the strands of her hair.

"Mom do you think we'll hear from Dad? He's been gone a year and a half."

Her mother stood up. "I don't know. I'll leave your door open," she added, turning away.

After dinner and after her homework was completed, Leeann placed sheets of newspaper across the kitchen table. On top she placed jars of oil paint, brushes, turpentine, and rags. She spread out a half dozen lead soldiers on the table. No more than four inches tall, some soldiers were mounted on horseback, some stood alone. She'd painted others a couple years ago with her father, but not these.

Her mother sat down at the table, careful to keep her coffee mug out of the way. "Tell me about these lead figures of yours. I've never asked you about them."

True, she had never shown interest. Leeann paused then picked up one. "This guy's a fifteenth century Persian soldier." She touched the tiny figure. "He's holding a shield in one hand and a lance in the other. He's also wearing a helmet." She looked at her mother. "There's a plume on top of that. He fought in the Middle Ages."

"His horse is wearing a blanket, I see."

"No, Mom, it's called a trapping. It's like a coat."

"I stand corrected."

Leeann put it back on the table beside the others.

"What is it about Persian soldiers you like?" She took a sip of coffee.

"I just like them."

"You've had them forever."

"When I was little, they were my toys. But Dad said these are collectors' items. We were starting to paint them."

"I'd like to paint one with you."

Leeann grinned. "Really?"

"Yes, I have a good eye for detail." She placed her mug in the sink.

"I have this one knight on horseback you can paint." She wiped it with a rag and handed it to her mother. "A knight was a nobleman who fought on horseback. He's holding a sword, and his horse is wearing plate armor. Yeah, you can do this one. I'd say he's one of my favorites."

For the next two hours, Leeann and her mother brushed shades of oil paint across the tops of horses' heads, across swords and armor and hooves, in creases and crevices, on helmets, lances and soldiers' faces. After a long stretch of painting, Leeann, squinted at the plume she'd just painted red. "When I was little, Dad and I used to line up my soldiers on the rug and have them fight against each other until every last soldier was dead."

"I'm not as good at painting as your dad, but how does this look?" She held up the miniature soldier for Leeann to inspect. Her mother's eyelids fluttered for a second, and she seemed to force them wide open, waiting for Leeann's response.

"Looks excellent, Mom."

CHAPTER 21

EASTERN MASSACHUSETTS, Boston and surrounding suburbs
1998

Traci warned Leeann not to go to Medina. She called the decision 'lunacy.' And still, Leeann climbed into her car on Monday morning. Her aching arm rested in a sling across her chest as she swerved off the exit to Karen Downey's house. She knew calling Ben would have been more sensible but instead, drove one-handed seventy miles an hour, weaving in and out of lanes, intent on confronting Karen.

Standing in front of Karen Downey's house, a wave of invincibility infused her. It was the twenty-seventh of April, and still, holiday garlands hung on her post-and-rail fence. An orange Buick with rusty fenders sat in the driveway. Its bumper sticker read, *Commit Random Acts of Kindness.* Leeann rolled her eyes. She moved a barrel blocking the front door and rang the bell.

"What do you want?" Karen, her hair soaking wet, looking as if she'd emerged from the shower, seemed surprised to see Leeann.

"Listen, Karen, this whole situation has gotten totally out of hand." Leeann folded her arms and widened her stance on the front landing.

The corners of Karen's mouth turned down. Her eyes looked tired and unfocused.

"I think maybe you're urging Eric to say things that aren't true." She paused to let her words sink in. "I did not cause the accident, and Eric admitted that when I brought him home to . . ."

"You have no proof."

Leeann stiffened. "Hear me out, Karen." She reminded herself to speak non-defensively. "Eric's changed his story since the day of the accident. Why? Because he's under pressure to lie. I think he wants to please you." Leeann smiled to show that she was intending to come across as friendly and unintimidating. Karen, dressed in a skimpy tank top and jeans, stood expressionless. "What you're doing is damaging to Eric. That's all I came here to say. You are hurting your son for life by making him lie." Finished with her statement, Leeann adjusted her sling and winced as pain shot through her shoulder.

"Seems you got into another car accident there." Karen pointed to Leeann's arm. "Hope you didn't hit another child on a bike."

"Tennis elbow, Karen."

Karen looked beyond Leeann. "Wait here, please. I want to show you something." She disappeared for several minutes. Karen returned and stepped onto the stoop. Before Leeann could blink, Karen had her arm in the air, pointing to something above Leeann's head, a bird or a tree or a cloud, she wasn't sure what. When Leeann looked up, she saw the pistol in Karen's hand.

"Whoa, whoa, whoa, Karen, put the gun down." Her heart seized.

"I've got a good aim. Can hit any target I want." She opened the barrel of the gun and showed that there were no bullets inside. "Did I scare ya?"

"If I made you feel threatened, Karen, I apologize. I did not come here to upset you." Leeann backed away. "But I see you're upset so I'll leave."

"Don't come here again," Karen said, through pursed lips.

"Didn't mean to offend you," Leeann said, using a fake deep voice, attempting to exude an air of superiority. She hurried to her car, got in, and gripped the wheel with her good hand. She peeled away, tires squealing, the engine roaring, her whole body shaking. She checked the rearview mirror, talking out loud to herself. "The woman's a nut, a certified crazy woman." She resolved to leave Karen Downey alone and decided to move to her backup plan.

The center of Medina reminded Leeann of the town she'd grown up in—the narrow downtown streets, the cluster of run-down stores on four corners of the intersection, men sitting on the porch in front of a drugstore. She went inside and got directions to Medina's middle school.

She pulled behind several cars idling in front of the school. Leeann was sure she'd recognize Eric Downey's round face, his shaggy hair, and slumped shoulders when he came through the doors. Was she out of her mind waiting to speak to Eric Downey? Adrenaline coursed through her body and made her lightheaded. She felt conspicuous, like a stalker. Her breathing became faster and deeper. Leeann removed the sling from her arm and tossed it onto the passenger seat. She unbent her arm and squeezed her fingers open and closed several times to get the blood circulating.

When several boys rushed out of the building, she got out of her car and asked a boy in a green shirt, "Do you know where I could find Eric Downey?" The boy shook his head and kept running. He yelled across the U-shaped driveway. "Walter, this lady's looking for Eric." Walter, with a black backpack hanging off his shoulder, walked over to Leeann. "Are you his Aunt Sandy? He's been trying to reach you."

"Can you help me find him?"

"He skips school a lot," Walter said, putting his backpack on the ground. "You can find him fishing off Ludlow Bridge. It's across from the hardware store in town."

Leeann waved a thank you.

Eric was not on the bridge, but under it. Leeann trudged down the steep embankment and walked up behind him. His fishing line was in the river, and a tackle box sat nearby.

"Hey, how are you doing?" Leeann asked.

Eric turned around with a grin on his face but his pleasant expression dissolved when he saw Leeann, and he turned away. He wore rumpled-looking blue jeans and a white polo shirt with a stain on the pocket.

She wondered when he last wore clean clothes. "What are you catching?"

"Trout."

Leeann looked around for a bucket of fish. "Where are they?"

"I throw them back."

"Catch many?"

"Yeah, I cast my line into that eddy over there behind the rock." He pointed to a boulder protruding from the middle of the river. "They like the calmness in the pool."

"Your friend Walter told me I'd find you here. He thought I was your aunt."

"What do you want?"

Leeann approached him, getting a closer look at Eric's rod and reel—they looked brand new—and the river—it was narrow and rocky. Eric's hair, pulled back in a messy pony-tail, rested on the collar of his shirt, and Leeann studied its snake-like shape, its coarse, faded, brown split hairs. He wore a diamond earring in his right ear.

"Well," she stammered, "I've been thinking a lot about you. We're alike in some way."

Eric stared into the water. "How so?"

"There was a time I told a lie because my father asked me to."

He turned to her. "Your dad told you to lie?"

"I didn't realize it then, but parents shouldn't ask their kids to lie for them. I don't like liars, and I didn't like being a liar. Know what I mean?"

The boy said nothing.

Leeann changed the subject. "Have you thought about college, Eric? You have to start working toward it now, going to school every day so you can have a great future. Maybe as a policeman or an engineer."

Eric kicked a couple of stones with his mud-stained sneakers. He turned and looked at Leeann. "My shop teacher says I'd make a good electrician. But I can't do it on my own."

Her tone turned gentle. "I know that, Eric. And I know your mom is having a hard time right now. You told me yourself that she's angry all the time."

Eric dropped his chin to his chest. He reeled in his line and cast it into the river, hitting the very center of the eddy.

"I think it would be smart for you to find your Aunt Sandy and tell her what's going on here with you and your mom. You can't fix this alone."

Eric released a loud exhale, startling Leeann. "Could you give me a lift home?"

Leeann shook her head. "Your mom would have me arrested for kidnapping."

Eric let out a laugh and quickly squelched it. "I'm out of water and I'm roasting. A mile walk is ahead of me." They walked to the top of the bridge and Eric continued pressing for a ride. "Please, I think I might pass out."

Leeann relented. "I'll take you close to your house and drop you off."

When Eric bent over to put his rod and tackle box in the back seat, a box of Newports fell out of his shirt pocket. Leeann grabbed them. "Give me those. You don't smoke cigarettes at fourteen years old."

Eric didn't argue. He got in the front seat, crossed his arms, and leaned back. Leeann tried to get a conversation going by asking him general questions about school, sports, and video games. Eric's replies consisted of some shrugs and a couple "I dunno's."

She asked him how he got started fishing, and that was the topic that brought life to Eric's eyes. He said he began watching this old man fishing off Ludlow Bridge about a year ago. The man showed him how to put bait on his hook and hold the rod and how to cast into the river.

"On days I didn't get detention, I'd bring a soda to him and stay and watch."

"So he taught you the basics."

"Yeah, then one day, the guy, Les, told me he was moving to North Carolina to live with his daughter and wouldn't be needing his rod and tackle box. So he handed them to me and I was like stoked. That's when I started fishing all the time."

"Did you ever hear from Les again?"

Eric squeezed his hands together. "No." After a long pause, he added, "Few months later, some guy in the drugstore told me Les died of cancer. He was never planning to go to North Carolina. He didn't even have a daughter."

"You're a really good kid, Eric."

"No, I'm a screw up."

"Les saw that you were a nice kid."

"We both liked fishing."

"You aren't a screw up," Leeann emphasized. "You should be going to school and you should not be smoking, and you are a great kid. I know that because you throw the fish back into the river." Leeann ran her hand across the steering wheel.

Eric stared at her with the same vacant look, the same red-eyed gaze Leeann saw in his mother earlier in the afternoon.

"Les used to do that."

Leeann pulled her car onto the side of the road one house away from Eric's.

"Can I have my cigarettes?"

"No," Leeann said, with a steady, I-mean-what-I'm-saying stare.

"I'll tell my mom you kidnapped me."

"I don't think you'll do that."

Eric jumped out. He grabbed his fishing rod and tackle box and, with an angry thrust, slammed the door closed. "You're in big trouble now," Eric screamed. He ran across his neighbor's lawn, almost running into the chain link fence separating their houses. Leeann put her hand up to the side of her head. She imagined the police showing up at her house again that night. She imagined herself being arrested, booked, and thrown in jail for god knows what Karen Downey will conjure up next. How could she have screwed up so badly?

Ben picked up Leeann's call on the fifth ring. "You sound upset," he said.

"I'm at a gas station. Can't hear you well."

Ben said he'd been at court all day working with clients who'd found no shortage of ways to mess up their lives. "I'm sitting on my balcony, looking at the Charles. There must be fifty sailboats cruising the water. What a sight. And I'm holding a glass of Shiraz. What's up?"

"I did something monumentally stupid."

"I'm holding my breath."

"Keep in mind that I haven't been myself. I'm losing control of my life. Traci's pursuing my father in California because of some stupid note sent to my hometown paper and I'm losing all my assets to Karen Downey."

"Leeann, slow down, you're making no sense."

"It may be perceived by some that I intimidated two witnesses today." She waited so long for him to reply that she had to ask, "Ben, are you still there?"

"Go on."

"Yesterday, a sheriff served me with a Complaint from Karen Downey. She's going after everything I've got. I went to talk to her. She pulled a gun on me, and then I might have kidnapped her son, Eric Downey. Ben, are you still there?"

"I'm here."

Leeann described her afternoon. "Can you help me?"

"I'm being transferred to the Cape Cod office so, I can't help you, but my boss can. His name is Sumner Smith and there's no way anyone can top him in the courtroom. He's fierce, and no one gets in his way."

"Sounds perfect."

"What you did today, Leeann, was insane."

"No argument from me."

"Now tell me about Traci and your father and this note. This is all new to me."

CHAPTER 22

WESTERN MASSACHUSETTS, Town of Berkshire Ridge
April, 1985
Leeann Bright, 14 years old

It was Sunday at last, the day Leeann would tell her mother the truth about the Mechanics Garage fire. She lay in bed, practicing the words out loud. "Mom, remember the night of the Mechanics Garage fire?" She forced sadness into her voice.

"I'm sorry I lied, Mom. Don't be mad at me."

She planned to confess at the Wexler Lake Art Fair. Her mother's mood was at its best walking outdoors in the sunshine.

They drove past the old stonewall at the intersection of Route Four and Farm Road. Leeann saw a green sign and read, "Wexler Lake, one mile." Her mother turned up the volume on the radio and sang along to the song, *The Lion Sleeps Tonight*. She was excited about the opening of her nursery the following week. "Everything is in place," she said. "We have new staff, and John Wicker will be back as assistant manager."

"Mom, I smell fried clams and French fries," Leeann said as they passed the Tucked Away Café.

"Honey, it's your imagination. The café is closed 'til next month. Have I mentioned John is wonderful with customers?"

"Yes, Mom."

"His knowledge of the natural world is impressive." She turned onto County Road and drove a mile until the road came to a dead end and another sign directed her to Beach Road. Wexler Lake, with its blue-green color, lay ahead. There were pine trees shooting high into the sky and pine needles on the ground.

A wide curving boardwalk, shaded by trees, hugged half of the lake. Colorful tents containing artists' paintings and photographs for sale were scattered along the length of the boardwalk. Children lined up to have their faces painted. Two women used a makeshift stage for a puppet show. Leeann pointed to a sign, "Free kites at one o'clock, Mom."

"We'll get you one. It's our day, honey. Today, I have no responsibilities except to have fun."

Leeann lugged beach chairs and a blanket to the lake's edge. Her mom followed with a canvas bag filled with sodas and snacks and sunglasses. Leeann came with nothing, other than her plan.

"Let's put our toes in the water," her mother suggested.

Leeann declined, distracted by the words swirling in her head.

"Why don't you run and get yourself some ice cream."

Leeann was occupying herself digging in the sand. Above her, the sky was blue, broken at one place with a scuffmark of white cloud. A crumpled, child-size, red umbrella skipped along the sand near the water, twirling with each gust of wind. Leeann retrieved it and brought it back to her chair. She fiddled with it, but tiring of that, tossed it aside. Her right leg bounced up and down. She rubbed her hand across her stomach, digging her fingers into her abdominal muscles.

"The stomachaches are getting less frequent, aren't they?"

Leeann was startled by her mother's voice. "Yeah, only once a month maybe." She pulled the bottle of pills from the back pocket of her jeans and held it up. "I don't go anyplace without them."

Her mother nodded. "Smart. Dr. Turtle says you'll out-grow them in time."

Although blankets and chairs littered the sand, most people were strolling the boardwalk. No one was within earshot of Leeann and her mother. And so, Leeann stood up and walked around the blanket, pretending she was looking for rocks. She picked up the red umbrella, examined it and again, tossed it aside. She settled back on the blanket near her mother and waited for her racing heartbeat to slow.

"Mom, I was thinking about…" But her voice, seized by emotion, faded. The sun moved behind the cloud, and Leeann felt a shiver go through her. Tears formed behind her eyes. She thought of Traci and how her life had changed in an instant the night of the fire. A tense breath lodged in her throat.

Her mother didn't seem to notice. "Look, there's John Wicker by that tent over there. Let's say hello." She was up and gone before Leeann could shake the sand off her hands. She got off the blanket and followed. Her mother, smiling, tapped John on the shoulder. He turned around and gave them a surprised-looking half-grin. They both commented on the weather, John saying you couldn't have asked for a better day for a fair, her mother saying that it seemed as if half the town had turned out for the event. Leeann wished she'd stayed on the blanket. Her mother chatted on. "Have you bought a painting? What time did you arrive? Are you here with anyone?"

John tapped a woman on the shoulder, and when she turned around, said, "Melissa, this is Helene Bright and her daughter, Leeann." Melissa, dressed in pink shorts, a white sweatshirt and two-inch sandals, flashed a smile. "I love your nursery. I've been in several times." She twisted a strand of her black hair around her finger, as if she was coiling a piece of twine around a garden stake. Helene fidgeted with her belt, no longer smiling, and nodded to Melissa. John covered his mouth and coughed.

"Leeann and I had better get going." Her mother put her hand on Leeann's shoulder and guided her, actually pushed her, toward the beach.

Leeann collapsed onto their blanket.

"I'm not feeling all that great, Leeann. I want to leave."

"Mom, you're upset. It's about that woman."

Her mother lifted the blanket at its corners. "I don't know her, but there are plenty of rumors going around. Let's just say she's not a person of good character."

"Mom, I don't want to leave."

Her mother slammed her sunglasses into her canvas bag. "Let's go."

"I'm having a good time here."

"It's too chilly to stay."

"They're giving out free kites."

"I'll buy you a damn kite. Now, get off the blanket."

"Why?"

"I don't want to be here, that's why."

Leeann's mother drove, gunning the engine after each stop sign. The car was silent, no radio or conversation. A mile down the road at the intersection of Route Four and Farm Road heading toward home, she made a sharp, rapid U-turn. She nearly skimmed the surface of a stonewall and grazed the forsythia bushes in front of it. Her face was red. She stopped the car.

"Mom, what are you doing?"

"We're going back." She looked out her window before pulling away from the shoulder and onto the road again. "I made a mistake. Yes, I'm annoyed at John, but those feelings shouldn't ruin our afternoon. We wanted to be at the lake today, so we're going back." She floored the gas, and Leeann's head jerked backward, bouncing off the car's headrest.

The breezes were strong at one o'clock. Leeann picked up her free kite at the entrance desk. Not far from where she stood on the sand, a dragon kite did cartwheels in the sky. A red kite in the shape of a bird took flight, then stalled in mid-air. It took a nosedive in to the sand. With her back to the wind, Leeann waited for a gust, and tossed her diamond-shaped kite in the air, watching it lift and stay airborne. She released the string and watched her kite fly higher. She took off running down the length of the beach, through the wind and beneath the sun. She could have been one of her lead figures, her 15th century Persian soldier, racing across the desert, white and scorched, in the center of Asia Minor. She ran over powdery granules of rock and mineral, over centuries of time. She ran from homework and curfews, from chores and rules, from the Mechanics Garage fire and Roland Barnes. She ran from the memory of her father, from her mother and the police. She ran from Traci and Norm Stylofski, and the lie she never confessed. Winded, she reached a place so far from the day that her sneakers flew high off the sand and the muscles in her face relaxed in a way they never had. She let out a whoop that scattered across the lake and beyond, maybe all the way to Persia.

CHAPTER 23

WESTERN MASSACHUSETTS, Berkshire Ridge
May, 1986
Leeann Bright, 15 years old

On a day she might have been playing volleyball after school with Traci and the girls from sophomore class, Leeann sat next to her mother on a bus to Springfield, checking the contents of her backpack: geometry book, gum, sunglasses. They were on their way to Springfield Medical Center. Her mother opened her Agatha Christie mystery book and flipped through it, searching for the page she'd last read.

"Why don't you get a bookmark?" Leeann asked. Her mother had always had a leaning toward orderliness. A bookmark seemed to be a necessity. Leeann was surprised her mother didn't have one.

"I'll do that," she responded, not looking up from her book. Meanwhile, Leeann counted the four hundred eighty-eight blue squares on the back of the cloth seat in front of her until she got bored and stared out the window. They drove through Fayeville and Macon, sparse towns of small wooden houses and tiny front lawns. Her mother looked up from her book.

"Oh, that weeping willow tree, look." Leeann had been admiring it too, from a distance. Its spreading branches reached downward and outward like a sweeping skirt. "When you see a weeping willow, you'll always see a body of water," her mother said, pointing beyond to Lake Hudson. "Their roots require huge amounts of water." Leeann pressed her face to the window. "That particular one is called *salix babylonica*. It's young, but it's going to grow to fifty feet high. Don't you love how it looks graceful and disheveled at the same time?"

Leeann nodded. Her mother's love of the natural world had become hers since she began working at the nursery. Her knowledge of everything green amazed Leeann. They stared out the window until the tree and the lake were out of view. Her mother opened her book and continued reading.

After her second dizzy spell that week, her mother had asked Leeann to accompany her to a doctor's appointment.

"So you're seeing another specialist?"

"When you don't agree with your doctors, you get a second opinion," she said, tapping hard on her opened book.

Leeann put a wad of bubble gum into her mouth and began chewing.

Her mother fixed her eyes on the seat in front of her. "Did you quit softball because of me?"

Leeann knew what she meant. She'd quit softball a few months earlier, on a day the crocuses shot through the ground announcing the start of spring. Her mother had been spending an increasing amount of time on the sofa during the day, and Leeann was helping John Wicker do more and more work at the nursery.

"No, I need time to study more."

"But you've been playing since you were eight years old."

"Mom, softball won't get me good grades and into college. I want a scholarship to Boston University."

Her mother grasped Leeann's hand. "You're a smart girl, Ms. Bright. It's good to have dreams and goals. Boston's a big, wonderful city."

"I know what I want, Mom. Softball is dumb."

"I think you should go back to it next year," her mother said, fingering her gold charm bracelet, which sparkled in the afternoon light. "Everything's going to be fine."

Leeann leaned back against the seat.

The bus stopped at a red light, at an intersection of Gaitlinburg Road and Stone Avenue. Leeann's eyes drifted left, to the railroad station, a decrepit structure decaying on its foundation. Seasons of grime and dust coated the shaky-looking building. A patch of weeds blocked its front door and rose to the height of the windows, which were cracked and broken and reflected a surrounding wasteland. Four crumbling pillars supported its gabled roof. It had once been the town's ornament, and now it languished. The light turned green and the bus accelerated toward the highway.

Leeann's mother closed her book and removed her glasses. "Leeann," she said looking at her daughter. "There are going to be more visits to the doctor."

"Yeah," she responded, looking down at the floor. It wasn't easy for a fifteen year old to talk to her mother about breast cancer. Leeann assembled her thoughts and questions in her head. "Are you going to get better?"

"Yes."

"Do you think we should find Dad and let him know?"

The mention of him startled her mother. She rubbed her eyes. The bus driver slammed on the brakes, and they both grabbed onto the seat in front of them. Leeann's backpack fell to the floor.

"He's gone," her mother pronounced. She lifted her head and took a deep breath. "Put him out of your mind."

"What do mean?"

"He's never coming home. It's been three years."

"He might if he knew you were sick."

Blotches the color of raspberry jam appeared on her mother's neck and spread across the skin below her collarbone, above the neckline of her dress. Her reaction was so personal, a silent reflection of her pain. Leeann didn't know where to look. Her vision contracted so that all she could see were her mother's eyes, tinged with the redness of fatigue.

"He's not coming back because of the fire, huh, Mom?" Her mother turned toward the window. "Because the police suspect him?" Leeann asked.

The bus bounced over a section of road under construction, causing her mother to grab her book on her lap.

"Do *you* think he did it?" Leeann asked.

"Daddy's not coming home because he felt tied down with us," she said, lowering her voice. "Your father never liked responsibility. He has his freedom now."

"But I'm asking you something," she whispered. "Do you think Dad left the tavern and set fire to Mechanics Garage?"

"I'll say it again, Leeann, put him out of your mind." She opened her book.

Forget him? She was telling her to move on, to not give a second thought to her father, to simply forget? The way one forgets the face of a reclusive neighbor or the ending to a dreadful book?

Thoughts collided in her mind. She'd believed for years that, as her father had said, the fire was an unfortunate mishap. But it was only recently she'd come to believe what the authorities declared, and not her father. The cause of the fire was arson.

Leeann watched as the bus exited the freeway and turned onto the main street of Springfield. Her mother pulled a hairbrush from her bag and ran it through her shoulder-length hair. A quick look in a tiny mirror confirmed that her lipstick was still colorful. Her bare arms looked white and delicate to Leeann, yet they were fiercely strong. Workers at the nursery joked that Helene could lift heavy boxes or pieces of equipment as easily as any man, and Leeann took pride in that.

The bus stopped with a lurch and the passengers stood up. Leeann was the first off the bus. The driver put out his hand and helped Leeann's mother down the steps. But Leeann had to run back to get her backpack, which she'd left under the seat in front of her. Now, the last one in line, she stepped off the bus and saw her mother standing on the wide sidewalk of Broad Avenue, her frail body a contrast to the towering State Building behind her. Her black sundress billowed like a sail in the breeze. Her mother curled her right hand and put it over her eyes, protecting them from the glare of the sun. Her shiny red lipstick outlined her lips and matched the tiny red hearts on her dress. The street was crowded with shoppers and tourists and downtown workers, who jostled her. One block away, St. Gregory's church bells sounded three times, each ring lengthened by a soft echo rippling over the city. With her hands still cupped over her eyes, Helene Bright turned toward the church steeple, as if drawn to the sound of the bells.

CHAPTER 24

WESTERN MASSACHUSETTS, Berkshire Ridge
May, 1986
Leeann Bright, 15 years old

Leeann spent the next day, Saturday, at the Berkshire Ridge Library finishing a term paper on factors that led to the start of World War I. She worked at a table beneath a circle of fluorescent lights. She took notes on a yellow tablet but wrote the final version of her paper on white paper with blue lines. Librarian Betty Ann Samuels sat nearby. Occasionally, Leeann got up and went to the reference desk to sharpen her pencil. She was careful not to make eye contact with Mrs. Samuels. It didn't take much to cause her to lose her temper—kids talking above a whisper, sneaking a soda into the library on a hot day, or wrinkling a page in a book by accident. She would reprimand by waving her wooden cane inches from a student's face. Leeann could get her friends laughing in a second by coming up with names for Mrs. Samuels. She'd refer to her as Captain Cranky or Ballistic Betty, but to her face, she was polite.

Leeann's view of the front door provided her with periodic distraction as she kept an eye on who entered the library. A teacher or a neighbor or someone from her mother's quilting class would enter, wave, and keep walking. She did not expect to look up and see Roland Barnes. He had a child with him, his grandson perhaps. She felt a wave of panic. She no longer talked to police and fire about the investigation into Mechanics Garage fire. She'd taken Roland's threats to heart and continued to look over her shoulder, fearing Roland Barnes would do something to hurt her or her mother.

With Roland's back to her—he was browsing the New Books display—she picked up her books and papers and headed to a remote corner of the library. On her way, she passed a shelf she'd never seen before. It contained telephone directories of major cities. She hugged the San Francisco book to her chest and brought it to a table. Her shoulders slumped when she found no listing for Richard Bright. She sat back and stared at the book. The back pages were yellow, and when she opened the book again, she saw that the back section contained listings of businesses in San Francisco. She flipped to a section called *Construction Companies*. There were dozens. She copied the names and addresses of each one. She composed the letter she would send to each company over the coming days.

Have you seen Richard Bright? He works construction. He's from Berkshire Ridge, Massachusetts. His family needs him. Dad, please call home. Your daughter, Leeann.

As Leeann was packing up to leave, Traci sauntered in, head down and carrying something that looked like a pet carrier. She approached Leeann, grabbed her by her blouse, and pulled her into a room beside the stacks of biographies.

"You got your cat in there?" Leeann asked.

"Something better."

"A puppy?"

"A bat. My sister caught it in our attic. I told her I had to show it to you."

Leeann squatted down to get a better look. "I see black fur but can't see his face."

"He's got real sharp teeth and teeny little eyes," Traci said, almost proudly.

"Wish I could get a better look." Leeann put her face close to the narrow openings of the carrier and squinted.

"Wouldn't it be funny if we let it loose right here?" Traci asked with a smirk.

"That would *not* be funny."

But Traci opened the door to the carrier, and when the bat burst out, Leeann fell back onto the floor. The bat soared above them. It flew out of the room and into the open lobby. They peeked out and watched the bat circle the reference desk, dive past a book cart, then soar upward. The screams from men, woman, and children were high-pitched, loud, and non-stop. People jumped over one another to get away from the bat. Some dove for cover under tables, others ran out the front door. Everyone had their hands over their heads. Mrs. Samuels swung at the creature with her cane. Someone shouted, "Call the Fire Department." Traci tossed the pet carrier under a table, and she and Leeann headed for the front door, but Mrs. Samuels blocked it with her cane.

"You girls stay right here."

Firefighters entered the building in minutes and used a net to catch the bat. Mrs. Samuels hollered that she'd seen Traci come walking into the library carrying something but never imagined it was an animal. She said she was calling the girls' mothers immediately.

Chief Gantry walked them outside. He didn't seem that mad. In fact, he told Leeann and Traci to get inside the fire truck and he would take them home. Traci froze in place. Leeann may have been the only person in the world who knew about Traci's terror of fire and anything related, like fire engines, sirens, campfires, and firefighters. But the chief helped lift Traci into the passenger seat, and Leeann followed. How cool was this to be riding through town in a fire truck. Leeann waved to several motorists. When she turned to give Traci a grin, she saw tears running down her friend's face. Her chest shook. Sobs followed.

"Letting a bat loose isn't the worst thing a kid could do," Chief said. "Don't feel so torn up." He patted Traci on the back. But the sobs and shaking continued. Traci's bottom lip curled over, her eyes squeezed shut. She didn't bother to put her hand over the waterfall coming down her face. Leeann placed her hand on Traci's back, while shooting a glare at Chief Gantry. Leeann figured that a smart fire chief would have guessed the source of Traci's emotions, especially because he and his lieutenant were the ones who carried Norm Stylofski's body out of Mechanics Garage. But Chief Gantry kept telling Traci over and over not to be so hard on herself, that it was only a bat.

Leeann breezed into her house. She moved around the kitchen opening the fridge, looking inside, opening cabinet doors, and slamming them shut, killing time and trying to avoid the inevitable confrontation with her mother. She strolled into the living room, where her mother lay on the sofa, watching *The Golden Girls* on TV. Like an old woman or an arthritic, her mother groaned as she pulled herself up and put her feet onto the floor. She pressed on her stomach with her fingertips, winced, and turned off the television.

"Still nauseous, Mom?"

"Yes, but I want to talk about *you*. Mrs. Samuels called. She's furious over what you and Traci did. It was immature and shameful."

Leeann sat on the edge of the chair. "I didn't do anything. Traci let the bat out on purpose. She's got a weird sense of humor."

"Listen Leeann, I believe you, and I'm too sick to punish you even if I didn't, but I want you to listen to me. Do not hang around with Traci Stylofski any longer." She picked up the bottle of aspirin and poured a pill into her palm.

"Why?"

"She's a troubled girl." Her mother popped the aspirin into her mouth and took a gulp of water.

"Troubled?"

"Rumors are going around that she steals from Mel's. And if that's not bad enough, the police found her on a bike on the far side of the reservoir at ten o'clock on a school night. There was a report of a break-in at a cabin over there, and police think it may have been Traci who tried to break in. Traci's mother didn't even know she was missing. She's trouble."

"Traci doesn't break into places. And she doesn't steal."

"You cannot hang around with the wrong crowd of kids, especially at your age."

There were days when Leeann wanted to avoid Traci because she reminded her of the fire. At the same time, she thought it was up to her to make Traci's life better. She would never walk away from her.

"I'm not going to blow her off, Mom."

"You tell her you've got to study harder because you're working toward a scholarship and can't see her any longer."

"I can't just drop her."

"I feel sorry for the girl." Her mother lay on the sofa, covering herself with a blanket. "Traci doesn't have a very bright future, poor girl." She placed a damp washcloth across her forehead and closed her eyes.

CHAPTER 25

EASTERN MASSACHUSETTS, Boston and surrounding suburbs
1998

The knock on the door was insistent. Leeann dropped the curtain she was hanging. She was alone in the house because Traci was having dinner with Jimmy. "Just to talk," she'd told Leeann. "I owe him that much."

Leeann opened the door to find Karen Downey on the other side.

"Hope I'm not interrupting," Karen said.

It was Friday, four days after their confrontation at Karen's house in Medina. "Well, actually, I'm preparing dinner."

"Can we talk?"

Leeann's voice lowered an octave. "You pulled a gun on me, Karen."

"That was nothin'. I was only trying to scare ya."

"What do you want?"

"You gonna invite me in? I'd like us to settle the lawsuit."

"No, and I'll see you in court, Karen."

"I look around," Karen sneered, "and observe the brand-new BMW in your driveway and your fancy mansion with pillars, no less. And I see you have a gardener. Much has been handed to you, Leeann Bright, like your fat salary. You ought not be so stingy. My son and I could use the settlement."

Leeann regretted opening the door. "It's evil of you to use your son in your phony scam." She reminded herself she should not provoke Karen and not escalate the situation. She wanted Karen Downey to go away. It made her sick thinking about going to court again. Maybe settling would be the smartest move. Yes, if Sumner Smith suggests she settle the lawsuit with Karen Downey, she would think about that.

Karen ignored the comment. "Twenty-five thousand, and we'll call it a day."

"I'll see you in court," Leeann snapped, but her stomach churned thinking about a trial and Karen possibly taking her life savings.

"I haven't heard from your attorney." Karen poked her head into Leeann's living room, directing her eyes to the crystal chandelier.

"You'll hear from him." Leeann closed the front door. She watched Karen walk across her lawn and stop in the middle of it, beside the lilac bush, its purple flowers swaying. The woman no longer appeared waif-like as she had weeks ago. Today, she looked tall and muscular, battle-ready, dressed in black and leather. Leeann drew the blinds. When she looked outside ten minutes later, Karen Downey's car was gone.

Leeann checked her spare bedroom on Saturday morning. Traci hadn't returned from her date with Jimmy. A good sign. She was hopeful the two were working things out. This couple should not be having problems. They belonged together.

Where did she belong? Where was her life going? She had no answers.

Leeann looked around the living room. She wondered why she surrounded herself with stark white walls. Why was she depriving herself of vivid colors and the pleasure of living with them? It wasn't just the white, but the bareness of the rooms in her house that bothered her. It suggested aimlessness, as if she had no intention of living there for long. The living room needed at least a bright, colorful print, maybe a Monet. Yes, a Monet. She would go with Impressionism.

Preparing to dress for the day, Leeann felt a sinking feeling as she flipped through her closet full of drab colored clothes. Bare white walls and bland, safe clothes, she chided herself. It's time for change. She thought too, of Karen Downey's words. "Your fancy mansion with pillars, your BMW, your fat salary." That's how Karen Downey defined her. If she only knew those things didn't bring Leeann happiness.

She spent the morning doing what she loved. She set up the automatic sprinkler, turned on the spigot on the side of the house, and let the water flow. If her arm hadn't been aching, she would have moved around the yard spraying roses, then the flowering bushes, then trees. She stood beside the sprinkler and let the water run down her hands and arms. Her jeans and sneakers got wet. The water flowed into the flowerbeds and pooled there before seeping into the ground.

On one side of the house in one curving bed, the mulch was thin because she'd run out and never finished the job last fall. She needed to buy mulch. Hemlock mulch. She usually went to the Acton Nursery Center. The clerks there knew her well. They often asked her for help. "We've got a parasite on one of our plants, Leeann. Mind taking a look?"

But Leeann had another plan. Today, she would buy Hemlock mulch at the Silver Sword Nursery in Haverhill, forty-five minutes from her house because Ben mentioned it was going to foreclosure. The thought of a new career had recently formed in her mind, and it now had Leeann walking on a cloud. Vivid walls and a snappy new wardrobe, and a new career path, she thought. These were changes long overdue.

The Silver Sword Nursery was located on the west side of Haverhill, where dense forests lined both sides of the road. It was two o'clock when she pulled into the nursery's nearly empty parking lot. One customer was milling around the hanging baskets of petunias in brilliant blue and magenta. No one lingered at the pots of white tea roses. Tables set up in front of the building were crowded with dozens of containers of impatiens and marigolds, all in need of attention. Lavender plants, waving their purple spikes, were for sale in a roped-off section, along with a variety of tired-looking bushes with cloth and rope wrapped around their root balls. Inside, there were few indoor plants. A man was examining samples of crushed stone. A woman was lifting a green gazing ball out of its box. Scattered about were patio tables and chairs and self-watering planters. A salesclerk in jeans and a red shirt was eating a sandwich behind a counter. On the wall was a two-foot by three-foot framed photograph of a Silver Sword. Its base was a tuft of silky, silvery leaves that looked like blades. A stalk grew out of its center and was covered with hundreds of flowers that looked like daisies. Experts called it a botanical wonder. Leeann could hardly take her eyes off it. She approached the clerk and asked for hemlock mulch, then asked if she could talk to the owner.

"Hold on, you're in luck. He's that man coming toward us." She stood up. "Dick, someone's here to see you." The man, gray-haired and middle-aged, stopped several feet away from them. He looked at Leeann through half-closed eyes.

"I'm Leeann Bright, and I heard through the grapevine that you might be looking for new owners. I was wondering what your price is."

"You interested in buying?" He walked toward Leeann.

"Someday, maybe."

"You come back someday, then." He walked away.

Leeann shot back, "Your marigolds have Botrytis Blight and it's a no brainer your impatiens have Downy Mildew."

The man spun around. "What do you do?"

"I'm a certified public accountant." She pushed hair away from her face.

Dick Perios, CEO of the Silver Sword Nursery and Garden Center, motioned to Leeann. She followed him to his office on the second floor. He removed yellowed, bulging files and offered Leeann a chair. "The place is in chaos," he mumbled. Perios leaned back in his chair and stared at Leeann. "You're a CPA who wants to buy a nursery. Why?"

"Because I'd be good at running it."

"The place is going to foreclosure. You'd buy it from the bank at auction."

Leeann sat up straighter. "It'll go to the highest bidder, in other words?"

"That's right. You're welcome to look over the books since you're here." He told Leeann he'd inherited the business from his brother three years earlier. "When you're not that interested in your work, it's easy to run it into the ground."

At the end of an hour Dick Perios asked, "You interested?"

Leeann took a few seconds to think over her reply. "I'm pretty certain I could make the business profitable." She didn't tell him she wasn't sure she wanted to quit her job right away, sell her house and move to Haverhill, Massachusetts, although Traci would love nothing more than to see Leeann living more north, closer to her house. Traci would do a dance knowing they could hang together more often. "Don't ask me to help out at your nursery," she'd say. "You know I'm no gardener."

"For starters you have to make loan arrangements with your bank ahead of time, and you've got to bring a ten-thousand-dollar cashier's check to the auction in order to place a bid." Perios walked Leeann outside. "And if you decide to move forward, you should get a real estate attorney to look over everything you're about to do." They shook hands. He made a grand gesture. "Go ahead, take a look around."

The woman in the red shirt insisted she be the one to place three bags of mulch in Leeann's trunk, while Leeann walked the grounds of the nursery, past shrubs, perennials, annuals, and ornamental trees. She walked into the woods, which lined the south side of the property where magenta-colored Alumroot sprouted alongside a stream. She saw beauty all around her, and in a strange way, that beauty gave her a surge of courage. She thought, starting immediately, she ought to stare fear in the face and do things she never thought she would do. Why not burst out of her malaise and get her blood rushing with excitement instead of terror? Why not face her fears and take a leap of faith?

Traci was at the table eating ice cream out of a half-gallon container. Leeann gave a spot check to the petals on her African Violets sitting on the windowsill. She plucked a few wrinkled blooms of dead growth from each plant, leaving fleshy little headless stems.

"How did everything go with Jimmy last night?"

"Well, it started out fine. We had dinner at Barney's, and then went to see *Titanic*. Great movie and Celine Dion's voice…amazing." She chowed down a large spoonful of ice cream. "But then we argued this morning. He said he'd adopt a kid alone if he had to."

Leeann sat down at the table across from Traci. "Why don't you pursue your search for my father, see if you can solve the mystery of the fire and your father's death. Get it behind you. Then you and Jimmy can work things out. Go to counseling, maybe."

"What? I could never spill my guts to a shrink."

Leeann took a deep breath. "I've made a decision. It will cheer you up."

"Not in the mood to talk. Not in the mood to be cheered up." There was an edge to her voice. "Mind leaving me alone?"

"I'll go with you to California." It was a decision Leeann made as a gift to her friend. There was no risk to her. Richard Bright would never admit he knew anything about the fire. He'll be clueless about the contents of the anonymous note. "Can't imagine why anyone would bring me into this," he would say.

Traci looked up and grinned. "I got an email from Uncle Ray telling me he heard from the jewelry shop owner in the Sunset District today. You know, that woman, Astrid Bloom? Richard Bright's gallery will be opening for business this coming weekend. She said she saw Richard walking past her store this morning, carrying boxes."

Leeann got up from the table and started a pot of coffee. She folded some hand towels and put them in a drawer.

"I'm thinking of going next Friday," Traci said, her mood seeming to improve. "For a long weekend."

"I could take a couple days off work too," Leeann said.

"Are you serious?"

"Yeah, really."

"I'm kinda dumbfounded but, thanks. I'm happy."

Leeann placed two coffee mugs on the table. "I had a visitor here yesterday evening," she said, letting out a huge sigh. "My new best friend, Karen Downey."

Traci stopped eating ice cream. "Tell me the whole story."

CHAPTER 26

EASTERN MASSACHUSETTS, Boston and surrounding suburbs
1998

It was sunrise on the second Friday of May when Leeann opened the sliding door to her patio and stepped into darkness. The landscape beyond was freeze-frame silent. Crows slept. Automobiles hunkered in their places. Morning dew coated lawns. In the midst of the stillness, she shook, thinking about Karen Downey. Put her out of your mind for now, she told herself. Talk it out with your new attorney after the trip.

In twenty-four hours, she'd be facing her father for the first time in fifteen years. She stood on her patio wishing she could change her mind about the trip. She felt like a character in a bad movie. How do you script a meeting with a father who abandoned you? "Hello, Dad. Did you forget to write me for the past fifteen years?" And what of their secret? "Do you remember you killed Traci's father?" She could almost hear the director shout, "Ready? Take your places everyone.

Action!" But there was no action that would bring a happy ending to this story. Leeann shook off her anxiety and tended to last minute details before the cab arrived to take her and Traci to Logan Airport.

"What if Karen Downey becomes one of these stalkers you can never shake?" Traci asked Leeann. "What if she never leaves you alone?" They were eating breakfast sandwiches at a table beyond the American Airline's security checkpoint. "This lawyer of yours better be good." Traci took the last bite of an egg and ham croissant.

"I'm in this mess because I stopped and helped a kid in the road." Leeann crushed her paper coffee cup and tossed it a distance into a trash barrel.

"Let's put Karen out of our minds and focus on what we're about to do in the next twenty-four hours, okay?" Traci said. "I'm excited and nervous. You?"

Leeann didn't answer.

"Do you think all that anger you have toward your dad will come spilling out when you see him?"

"That's not my style," she said. "But anything's possible, I guess."

Traci continued to press. "They say it's unhealthy to keep your anger bottled up inside for years. It can make you sick. Maybe you ought to confront him for walking out. But not right away. I need to get my answers first."

"I have only one emotion right now and it's all I can deal with. Fear. No, terror."

"Oh, Leeann, I'm sorry," Traci said. "Fear of what?"

"Of how I'll feel seeing him again."

With boarding passes in hand, they headed for gate fourteen. Traci checked the contents of her backpack for her ticket, extra cash, and ID. She'd gone through it three times already that morning. Now, at concourse A in front of the Lobster Pot restaurant, Traci stopped again to check the contents of her backpack.

Leeann caught on. "This isn't easy for you either."

"I'm obsessing over my ticket and wallet because I'm scared stiff to get on this plane."

Leeann put her hand on her friend's shoulder. "The trip means a lot to you, doesn't it, Traci?"

"I've been waiting to do this, and now I'm not sure if it's the right thing."

Leeann assured her, "We're in this together. Try to relax."

"Okay, but just one question. You think the grounds people rifle through suitcases and steal things?"

"Stop worrying," Leeann answered.

"I haven't thanked you for taking the trip with me," Traci said, giving a quick glance at her friend. "Why'd you decide to come?"

"Insanity." They queued up to board the plane.

Once seated, Traci gripped the arms of her chair, digging in her fingernails. "Talk to me. Distract me." Grinding sounds emanated from the engine. She stiffened and grabbed Leeann's hand. The lights flickered on and off.

"I was supposed to call Ben last night," Leeann began. Traci kept her eyes down and leaned back in her seat. "He called last week to see how I was doing with the Karen Downey mess, and I brought him up to speed."

"Nice of him."

"Moron that I am, I forgot to call him back. Totally forgot."

Traci nodded, as if she were agreeing with the moron part.

Passengers wedged into seats around them. The color drained from Traci's face as the plane roared down the runway, lifted, and banked.

"Look down there," Leeann insisted. "You'll see your work all over the city. There's the cable bridge you worked on, the high-rises in the Seaport District, and over there is the Financial Center."

"It's not helping, Leeann, I'm in full blown panic mode."

"How can a woman who works on skyscrapers be afraid of heights?"

"Not heights, planes. It's not natural for a seven hundred-thousand-pound aircraft to hang in the sky."

"It's not hanging. The wings create a lifting force that keeps the plane airborne as long as it's moving. It can't fall out of the sky. Picture it resting on heavy air or on water."

Traci closed her eyes. Beads of perspiration covered her forehead.

The city lights behind it, the plane banked sharply over rural Massachusetts and flew above the western part of the state.

"Down there somewhere is Berkshire Ridge," Leeann said.

Beyond the thick square of glass, the ground came into view: neighborhoods of tiny boxes bathed in stark sunlight, lakes and farmland, forests and meadows. Leeann fought to keep her own fears from consuming her. She wondered about her father. Did he still repair automobiles? Did he have more children? What books did he read? Was he lonely? Did guilt haunt him? Was he sorry?

Calming the thoughts in her mind, she turned to Traci. "Do we have a game plan?"

"I do." She looked less pale than she had a few minutes before. "We tell Richard we found him on the Internet and decided to stop by on this West Coast trip we'd been planning for months. We can't pump him in his store, so we offer to take him out to dinner. We move into the stuff about the fire and the note at the end of the meal."

Leeann nodded.

"You must have a ton of questions you want to ask him," Traci added.

"Not really." But she thought to herself, yeah, I do have a few questions for him. How was life without Mom and me? Did you think about us? Did you get what you wanted out of life? Was it all worth it?

Somewhere over the Midwest, over the Great Lakes, Traci reached inside her jacket pocket and pulled out a business size envelope. She opened it and took out a piece of paper.

"Is this the infamous anonymous note?"

"Yeah, I thought your dad might want to see evidence that someone was accusing him of knowing stuff. He might recognize the handwriting."

Leeann loosened her seatbelt and inhaled deeply. "I still think the note's written by a man. Maybe someone pissed at my father."

"I'm going to find out."

"I have a new hunch who wrote it," Leeann said. A spell of turbulence caused her to stop talking and fasten her seatbelt. She waited for it to end, then continued. "One of the detectives investigating the fire was John Handley. He occasionally called my mother to see how she was doing after my father left town and to make sure I wasn't stowing away on any more planes. The other day, Handley popped into my head."

Traci added, "He seemed to care about solving the crime. He'd call my mom, too, with occasional updates about the investigation."

"Handley was an old geezer fifteen years ago. He must be quite old now," Leeann said.

"He hasn't been on the force in over a decade," Traci replied. "My sister told me he's long been retired."

"I'll look up Handley when we get back. Go see him, maybe."

"Didn't think you really cared who wrote the note."

"I think about it occasionally." She had another hunch but didn't share that with Traci. She thought John Wicker might have written the note. He and Leeann's mother had been close, possibly romantically involved. It was easy to think that Leeann's mother had confided her belief that her husband was responsible for the fire. John ran the nursery for four years after Leeann's mother died. After he married, he moved to Tampa, Florida, to start a landscaping business. The last thing Leeann wanted to see was Traci marching down to Tampa to look up John Wicker and ask him what he knew.

The sun spread daylight over the wings of the plane, filling the cabin with warmth. After six hours, the captain's voice came over the loudspeaker. "You might want to take a look out the window. Mighty nice views." Leeann put aside her magazine. She was glad she'd chosen the window seat. She glanced at the sight of land and water, then the inlets and bays, with their outstretched fingers. The sky was a vibrant blue, the color of precious stones, but nothing got her heart rattling more than the frigid, unblemished, green-blue Pacific Ocean below.

CHAPTER 27

WESTERN MASSACHUSETTS, Berkshire Ridge
April, 1987
Leeann Bright, 16 years old

Maybe it was the way the girls raved about the new coach, Madeline Holly, or because Leeann's old team won the softball state championship, thanks to the new coach's strategy. Perhaps it was because her mother insisted she play sports again. In April of Leeann's junior year, softball drew her back.

Coach Maddie faced Leeann in the dugout one afternoon before the other players arrived. "You're a solid hitter, Leeann."

"Thanks. I haven't played in a year. I'm rusty."

"Come to the field a half hour before practice every day. I'll get you in shape."

Leeann rubbed linseed oil over her glove, and when she finished, cleaned Coach Maddie's glove, too. When she pulled a handkerchief from her back pocket to mop her sweaty brow, her bottle of pills fell to the ground. Coach Maddie picked it up.

"What's this?"

"Medicine for stomachaches."

"Prescription?"

"Yes."

"There's no pharmacy label."

"I get them from Dr. Turtle."

"What are they?"

Leeann shrugged.

"They're not labeled, they don't come from a pharmacy, and you've got no idea what you're taking? You doing street drugs?"

"No, it's medicine. I haven't needed it in a year, but I carry it on me."

The coach smelled the pills. She stared at the bottle, turning it over in her hand. "You're sixteen, you should know what you take."

"I was never told."

"Mind if I keep them for a few days?"

"I'm not lying, Coach Maddie."

"I hate to sound mean, but you know the rules. You're off the team if this crap is illegal."

"It's not illegal."

Leeann couldn't move. She was stunned her coach didn't believe her. She caught her breath and raced to meet Traci and Lynn, who were running toward her with their gloves tucked under their arms.

At practice, three days later, Leeann straddled the foul line near home plate. She stretched her bat over her head as Coach Maddie approached. Her walk was casual, not the brusque, cut-to-the-chase way she usually moved.

"You can have your pills back, Leeann. Coach handed her the bottle. "The pharmacist over at Mel's tells me they're sugar pills."

Leeann raised her eyebrows.

"Do you know what a placebo is?" Coach Maddie waved the bottle. "Because that's what you've been taking for your stomachaches."

Leeann groped for a response but words wouldn't come. Her face felt hot.

"Don't be embarrassed. They must have made you feel better."

"Guess I should throw them out."

"I apologize for doubting you, Leeann. Really, I am sorry." Coach Maddie started to walk away, then turned back. She gave Leeann a hug. "You're really a great kid. I admire all you're doing for your mom and that you achieve good grades, and still have time for sports."

Leeann took in the Coach's words, the warmth of her touch. She nodded.

Coach Maddie shouted, "Okay everyone, line up for batting practice."

Leeann didn't throw away her pills. She put the bottle in her back pocket and brought it home. She had a newfound admiration for her mother and Dr. Turtle for having pulled one over on her for four years. They knew the suggestion of a pill would stave off her stomachaches. She never guessed she wasn't taking honest-to-god medicine.

She wondered what else her mother might be keeping from her. Over the next couple days, Leeann developed a curiosity about the file cabinet in the spare bedroom. She'd never looked in it and now wondered if there were other secrets about her hidden in the drawers. On Saturday, when her mother left the house, Leeann slipped into the spare room and stood in front of the two-drawer cabinet. She ran her hand over its metal surface. The grooves on the front of the drawers served as handles. She tugged on the top one and it glided out. Inside were stationery supplies—pens, pencils, envelopes, paper, and more. She pulled out the bottom drawer to find file folders. They were labeled insurance, jury duty, Leeann's birth certificate, dental, medical, banking, taxes and legal. She flipped through them and found nothing relating to her other than her birth certificate. The folder labeled "medical" contained her mother's blood test results. She went back to the legal folder, and inside, came across a business envelope. The return address read "Connors and Pesterfield, Attorneys-at-Law, Market Street, San Francisco, California. Leeann spread the papers in front of her on the floor. She didn't understand their meaning. She read the cover letter once and again a second and third time. Leeann dropped her head into her hands. They were divorce papers. Her father had filed for divorce. "You bastard," she whispered. She filled with rage thinking of the time she wasted writing to construction companies in San Francisco trying to find him. "You bastard," she repeated. The papers were dated two years earlier and remained unsigned.

She returned the documents to the folder and closed the drawer. Her mother wouldn't be home for another hour.

Leeann collected the items her father had sent her for Christmas a few years back: a key chain with a miniature baseball bat attached to it, a game of Monopoly, a pair of sunglasses and a Polaroid camera, and dumped them in a paper bag. She paced around the house, raging that her father no longer wanted anything to do with her or her mother. Leeann went to her room and scooped up the two dozen lead soldiers she'd gotten as a gift from her father at one of the yard sales they used to explore. They went into the paper bag, too. She crumpled the bag and put that in a plastic bag, which she dumped in the trash barrel beside her house.

She wanted to go to the fire chief and tell him who set fire to Mechanics Garage but was stopped by a truth never far from her mind. In keeping quiet for four years, she was covering up a criminal investigation by lying and protecting her father. That made her a criminal, too. She could never tell.

CHAPTER 28

WESTERN MASSACHUSETTS, Berkshire Ridge
May, 1987
Leeann Bright, 16 years old

S pring softball season was a distraction from her mother's illness. Games and practice, along with errands, chores, and homework took up all of Leeann's time. Others helped. John ran the nursery, and Grace and Lee from church cared for her mother during the day. They drove her to doctors' appointments, prepared meals, and on beautiful days, took her to visit the botanical garden in the neighboring town of Windsor. The three of them often stopped by the nursery. "See, it's running efficiently," Lee would say. Her mother smiled when she saw crowds of people heading toward the cashier's shed. Grace, who was Coach Maddie's sister, and Lee would buy freshly cut Blue Iris for Helene to place on a table in the living room.

One Saturday, while Grace was visiting, Leeann slipped into the kitchen through the back door to grab her softball bag. She stopped when she heard her name mentioned. Her mother's voice quivered. "Grace, I don't know what to say. Leeann's math teacher, Mrs. Sanders, has offered to let her stay with her until Leeann leaves for college."

"Maddie would love to have Leeann stay with her," Grace said. "They know each other well, and Maddie adores your daughter. If you are open to it, my sister will come and talk to you."

"I'll have to run it by Leeann, but thank you, Grace."

Leeann left the house shaken, and marched along the side of the road with her head down, almost crashing into a kid's wagon in a driveway.

That night, Leeann's mother asked her to turn off the TV. "I want to talk about the future. *Your* future." She lifted a cup of tea to her lips. Both hands steadied the cup. Leeann cringed, knowing what was coming. "As you know, I'm starting an experimental drug. We're certain it's going to work, but I need to plan for the worst." Leeann gripped her hands in her lap. "I'm going to beat this."

"I know you are, Mom."

"Grace says her sister Maddie Holly and her husband want you to live with them if something should happen to me. They live on Loker Road and have a son and a swimming pool." She buttoned the top pearl button of her sweater. "You'll be well cared for until you to leave for college."

Leeann suppressed a smile. "Coach Maddie? Yeah, great." She retreated to her room, kicking aside books and clothes strewn about on her floor, and flopped onto her unmade bed. She shuffled a deck of cards from her nightstand and sprayed them across her room. The guilt from that flicker of enthusiasm she felt about living with Coach Maddie left her numb for hours.

CHAPTER 29

WESTERN MASSACHUSETTS, Berkshire Ridge
December, 1987 and April, 1988
Leeann Bright, 17 years old

Doctors were optimistic when Helene Bright's cancer went into remission. The experimental drug seemed to be working.

Helene was cautious. "Let's not jinx things by getting excited."

But Leeann knew her mother was totally excited. She began reading books again and listening to music. It was Christmas, and Maddie and her husband Mike set up a Christmas tree in Leeann's living room. They decorated it with garlands and tiny lights. They bought presents for Leeann and her mother and placed them, wrapped in foil and bows, under the tree. On Christmas Eve, a new driver, Leeann drove her mother around Berkshire Ridge looking at Christmas lights and decorations on the town green.

Winter passed with what seemed like a snowstorm every week. By the end of March, temperatures warmed, and crocuses sprouted across the Bright's front yard. Leeann and her mother celebrated the advent of spring with the news that Leeann had been awarded a full scholarship to Boston University. It was a busy time for her, keeping up her grades, playing softball, and taking her mom to chemotherapy appointments. But things were changing. John Wicker and Mike moved her mother's bed to the middle of the living room. Chemotherapy was discontinued. An attorney visited with papers for her mother to sign.

"Why is Maddie taking your books?" Leeann asked.

Her mother waived a frail hand. "I've read them all. It's time to share them with someone else."

In April, the day of a big game, Leeann's mom was discharged from the hospital after a set back from dehydration. Leeann watched as nurses hugged her, tears in their eyes.

Leeann made it to the game. It was over ninety degrees that afternoon at Waters Field. The heat had been relentless for a week, and now the humidity arrived. Players' sweat dripped down their faces and onto the balls and bats. Berkshire Ridge Leopards and the Vernon Tigers were tied. It was near the end of the ninth inning, and the rival team was at bat. Rhonda Fitzgerald slammed a solid hit and took off running, making it to first base. The ball flew toward Leeann. She didn't move, didn't turn around to see where the ball landed, and didn't run to pick it up. She didn't see Rhonda circling the bases. She'd entered her own circle of time and space. Her gloved hand dangled at her side. She heard voices shouting, "Get the ball, Leeann. Throw the ball. What's wrong with her?"

Leeann's feet remained planted to the grass. It was Jan Wilson, Josh's sister, who ran from left field and threw the ball home. But Rhonda had already scored the winning run. Traci pitched off her catcher's mask and raced to Leeann's side. "Hey, what's the matter?" And when Leeann didn't answer, Traci walked her off the field.

Hailey Lambert, who pitched a great game for Berkshire Ridge, was furious. "You choked, Leeann, and lost the game for us."

"Ever hear of heat stroke, you moron?" Traci hollered.

While Leeann's teammates congratulated the winning team, Coach Maddie took Leeann inside the dugout and filled her with Gatorade. "Lie down."

Leeann protested. "I'm fine, except for being a screw-up."

"The heat gets to everyone," Coach Maddie said. "It's okay."

The Coach let Leeann ride her bike home, as long as Traci stayed beside her. They stopped at Mel's Café. Leeann waited on the porch while Traci bought sodas for both of them.

"I didn't have heat stroke," Leeann said, when Traci returned.

"I know. You were in a trance. What were you thinking?"

Leeann lifted her head to the sky. She blinked hard. "My mom is gonna die."

Traci put her hands on top of her head. They stood in silence for a few minutes.

Leeann watched Traci take sips from her soda can, watched Traci's eyes wander and not meet hers. "Let's go home," she said.

Days later, Leeann's mother's oncologist, Dr. Joseph Batten, Chief of Oncology at Springfield Medical Center, sat down with Leeann in a sprawling office overlooking an azalea park in bloom, and told her what she already knew. "The experimental drug we've been giving your mother is no longer working. The prognosis is not good."

CHAPTER 30

CALIFORNIA, Sunset District
1998

The GPS in the rental car directed them to Seaside Road in the Sunset District. Leeann and Traci stood in the doorway of Rachel's Bookstore, across the street from the Bright Art Gallery and Tang Frame Shop, a single door serving as entrance to both. They looked like tourists strolling down the street in their capris and jelly sandals.

Leeann clutched the flesh of her neck.

"It's now or never," Traci said. "Let's go."

They crossed the street and entered. The gallery was empty except for a man with his back to them, talking on the phone. Traci elbowed Leeann in the side. "It's him."

Leeann held her breath until the man turned around and whispered, "I'll be right with you." It wasn't Richard Bright, but a balding Asian man who looked to be in his forties. He was wearing a white dress shirt, sleeves folded at the elbows, his arms stippled with paint in various colors. He wiped his hands with a rag. Still on the phone, he ducked into a back room. Leeann poked her head into the other half of the store, the frame shop, and saw it too, was empty.

The walls in the gallery were painted cranberry. Hardwood floors glistened. Leeann circled the room. "Check this out. Paintings of automobiles."

"Trucks and motorcycles too. They cover two gigantic walls," Traci added.

Leeann's gaze settled on one, a classic Pontiac sedan in deep green with rally wheels, chrome bumpers and a running board. On another wall were paintings of bodies of water. Blue and white brush strokes swept across canvasses in scenes with big skies and cresting waves. "Seems Richard likes painting bodies of water, too.

The man returned. "May I help you?"

Leeann stammered, "We'd like to meet Mr. Bright."

"I'm sorry, no," the man said. "He's in the city today. He does much of his painting there." The man enunciated his words with precision.

"We'll look around," Traci said.

"Please," the man replied, extending his arm in a sweeping gesture. He said his name was Phillip Tang, and he was the manager of both shops.

Leeann examined paintings, stalling for time, planning her next move. She read the text panels on the walls beside the paintings. Traci did the same. When Tang passed them again, Traci spoke up. "We're going into the city. Where would we find Mr. Bright?"

"He has meetings all afternoon."

"He started painting later in life, is that right?" Traci asked, folding her arms and facing Tang.

"Yes, in his forties." He dusted one of the frames with a rag.

"He's from the East Coast, isn't he?"

"Yes, Massachusetts."

"Is he married?" Traci asked, and then glanced at Leeann, who turned her back and shook her head.

"No, unmarried."

"Mr. Tang, are you a good friend of Mr. Bright's?" Traci asked.

"I've known him for a long time. And you ask because…"

Leeann spun around, facing the two. "She's asking because my name is Leeann Bright. I'm Richard's daughter."

Tang's wide-eyed expression remained unchanged for what seemed like an eternity. He studied Leeann's face through round, rimless glasses.

"My god," he said, holding the sides of his face with his hands. "My god, my god." He grabbed Leeann's hand and squeezed tight.

"Will you help me find my father?"

"I've known Richard for fifteen years. He has spoken of you."

"This is my friend, Traci Stylofski." They shook hands.

"Of course, I will take you to see Richard tomorrow."

"When you say 'take us to him,' can you be more specific?" Leeann shifted from one foot to the other.

"I can't say, but you will see him. I guarantee you will see him." Tang stared at Leeann. "I'm pleased to meet you." He paused to remove his glasses and wipe his forehead with the back of his hand.

"Is there any way we could see him today or tonight?" Traci asked.

"Not possible." Tang pressed his lips together. "Meet me in Memorial Park in downtown San Francisco at ten o'clock tomorrow morning. On the Jefferson Avenue side, there are some benches." He turned to greet three women who entered the store. "I can't say more."

"We'll be there," Leeann said, but she wanted to stay and ask Tang more questions. Instead, she followed Traci to the door. "Do you think he'll be willing to see us?"

"He'll have no choice," Tang replied.

Once outside, Traci repeated Tang's words. "He'll have no choice." She scratched her head. "Doesn't sound promising."

"Why couldn't he say where he'd be taking us?"

"There's something odd about this," Traci mumbled. "Don't you think this is like freakin' odd?"

CHAPTER 31

WESTERN MASSACHUSETTS, Berkshire Ridge
May, 1988
Leeann Bright, 17 years old

Helene Bright lay in the open ward of the hospital, fans circulating stale air as she fought pneumonia. It was two weeks before Leeann's graduation, and she visited her mother each day, eating cafeteria food for dinner and going home to an empty house. During the day, women from church kept her mother company. They looked out for other patients too, when they needed a sip of water or help removing the lids on their soup bowls or glasses of milk.

Leeann's mother spent her days in bed, half-buried beneath a cotton blanket even though the ward was ghastly warm. Leeann would fluff up her pillows to make herself useful, and she'd close the blinds when the sun streamed in and made the ward stifling. Leeann's mother responded each time with a nod. She didn't speak often. Nurses wheeled groaning patients past Leeann on gurneys. All around her, machines beeped, and the smell of ammonia lingered in the air each time the floors were washed. Across the room a patient, a man with silver, slicked back hair, sat stiffly, like a wooden soldier, in his wheelchair and watched Leeann.

On Wednesday afternoon, her mother bolted upright in bed. "Leeann, I knew you'd be here." The intravenous antibiotics had fought the infection that had caused her lungs to fill. Her face was pinker, her eyes brighter. She'd rebounded from the pneumonia, and Leeann was told she would go to a nursing home by week's end. Her mother reached for her hand. "Why don't you read to me? Read something you've got in your book bag."

"*Boswell's Life of Samuel Johnson?*"

"Yes, I want to hear your voice. Speak nice and loud," she murmured.

"Mom, I don't think everyone in the ward wants to hear this."

The silver-haired man in the wheelchair cranked his neck forward, as if signaling his wish to be wheeled closer to Leeann. His two hands held onto his suspenders.

"Yes, they do. Speak up, now."

Leeann pulled her plastic chair close to her mother's bed. Boswell and Leeann entertained her mother and the silver-haired man well into evening. The man in the wheelchair eventually fell asleep in the same corner where he'd been sitting for hours. Leeann kissed her mother goodnight. "I'll be back tomorrow, Mom."

Leeann's sleep was fitful. She woke in the middle of the night. Her mind was taunted by images of needles piercing her mother's blue veins, of oxygen tubes making sucking noises and caskets buried deep in the ground. She envisioned cells eaten by cancer and flowers multiplying out of control until thousands filled her mother's hospital room, surrounding her weightless body. Crazy thoughts. Leeann lay awake, wanting to leave the earth with her mother. Around three, she welcomed the familiar signal of sleep about to come: a wave of grogginess overtaking her, as if a switch had been thrown in her brain. She fell into a deep rest.

Leeann was sitting in the first row next to the blackboard. She'd just answered a question about *A Tale of Two Cities*. Mrs. McShane, the assistant principal, entered the room. It was ten thirty. She didn't look at the students but went directly to Leeann's teacher and whispered in her ear. Mrs. McShane approached Leeann and asked her to come with her to the principal's office. Leeann knew why she walked through the empty hallway behind her. She knew when she entered the principal's office and saw Coach Maddie. She knew when the Coach hugged her and said she was so very sorry.

"Leeann, your mom died peacefully early this morning."

Leeann put her hands over her eyes and cried. Coach Maddie helped her walk out of the building, putting her arm around Leeann's waist to keep her from stumbling across the grass to her car.

"Where is my mother?" Leeann asked through sobs. "What happens now?"

"She'll be taken to the funeral home."

"Do we plan her funeral?" Leeann wiped her eyes with her sleeve. "Will I get to see her one more time?"

"Remember, your mom didn't want a funeral?" Coach Maddie responded. "She wanted her ashes spread on the Piscataqua River in the town in New Hampshire where she grew up."

CHAPTER 32

CALIFORNIA, San Francisco
1998

The aroma of sugar and cinnamon drew Leeann and Traci into the Sunrise Bakery. Traci pointed to a glass case of pastries. "Bear claws and hot coffee. Let's order." They maneuvered their trays through a tight path between tables to find seats at the window.

"Did Tang seem credible to you?" Traci asked, before taking a first bite.

Leeann mumbled with her mouth full. "Mysterious, maybe."

"You think he'll show up or stiff us?"

Leeann shrugged and pointed to her pastry. "Eating here. No more questions. I'm more nervous today than yesterday."

A ceiling fan forced waves of cool air on them. Leeann handed Traci the Sports section, and she scanned the front page of the *San Francisco Chronicle*. A headache formed over her left eye. She thought of Richard's greeting, if it took place at all, and feared it would be as uninviting as a case of malaria. Her father, she predicted, would turn to her and ask what the hell she wanted after all these years. How would she answer that? Still, she was certain her father would never admit to the fire. She was sure she didn't have to worry about that. Leeann calmed herself remembering she and her father loved each other once. They'd built fences along their property, created a tree house in the backyard, gone on motorcycle rides to Wexler Lake. She wondered if her father loved baseball the way he did years ago when they drove two hours to Fenway Park. She wanted to recall the last words she'd said to her father, the last meal they shared, but instead, she buried her head in the comics.

They entered Memorial Park on the Jefferson Avenue side through a wrought iron gate a little before ten. There was no sign of Philip Tang. Leeann let the smell of cut grass lift her up and away from the acid turning in her stomach. There was no glimmering sun overhead, no brightness through the leaves. There were only thick clouds casting grayness over the park, over the rolling hills, the clumps of trees, and forsythia bushes. A woman sat on a bench, a baby carriage by her side. In the distance, a boy called out as he ran after a black lab, a man lounged on the grass, and a couple on a blanket sipped from a thermos. Farther off, a woman stood gazing at a tree. Leeann thought how common it was for people to pause and admire trees in spring and summer and particularly in fall. But her favorite time of year for studying trees was winter. She lost herself in the curves and dips of their branches when they were bare. She loved the rough brown bark, the hearty limbs, some gnarled, some smooth and lean. She admired the way one side of a tree mirrored the other. The true beauty of a tree's shape, its uniqueness and symmetry could be seen only in winter when it was exposed, she believed.

They sat on a bench and waited for Philip. Traffic clogged the surrounding streets, and behind them were red brick apartment buildings. Leeann wondered if Richard lived in one of them and if he was there inside, waiting for them now. Traci checked email on her phone. "Jimmy sent us a good luck message," she said.

Leeann circled the bench. She felt as if a sea of time between her childhood and the present had washed away. She was twelve again, waiting for her father to come home.

Appearing in a white dress shirt and jeans, Philip Tang greeted Leeann and Traci at ten. Phillip gripped Leeann's hand with a handshake that belied his meager build, throwing her off guard when he drew her in for a hug. He did the same with Traci. They sat down. Phillip removed his glasses and wiped them with a handkerchief.

"How are you both doing?"

"We had dinner last night on Fisherman's Wharf," Traci said.

Leeann added, "We toured the Asian Art Museum and rode cable cars."

Traci got down to business. "We *are* going to see Richard this morning, right?"

"Yes, but first we must talk." Philip put on his glasses and pushed them against the bridge of his nose. He scanned the park before turning his attention to them.

"Could we talk while walking?" Leeann asked. She held out her hands, palms upward. "Looks like rain any second."

"No, we must talk here."

Leeann glanced at Traci, who gave her a don't-ask-me-what's-going-on shrug.

Philip leaned forward, his elbows resting on his knees, and looked ahead as he began. "Richard and I have a long history. He has been a tenant of mine for fifteen years. We became friends after his construction accident ten years ago. He was incapacitated and bored, and so I brought him some paints and brushes. He was a natural right away. He's self-taught."

"He never had an urge to paint back home," Leeann added. "This is a real surprise to me."

"When he recovered, he was too disabled to go back to construction. He did odd jobs to make money. In his spare time, we'd play cards and go fishing. But his passion for painting consumed him."

"Talk about a late bloomer," Traci piped up.

"He was. And he was a good friend when my wife got sick five years ago. When I had to be away, he took her to doctors' appointments and rushed her to the hospital several times. After she died, I offered to help him start a business with his paintings to repay him for what he'd done for us. I gave him half my store and ran ads in magazines. His business went well for a year. Then his problems started again." Philip paused and took a deep breath. "Richard is a sick man."

"Is he in the hospital?" Traci blurted.

"No, Richard is an alcoholic. There are periods when he doesn't come home for days at a time, particularly in summer. He hangs out wherever he can. When the weather gets cold, he lets me take him to the VA hospital. Last night I went to several shelters to find him and tell him you'd come to see him. I couldn't locate him. But I know where he goes every morning when he's in this state."

"Are you kidding me, Philip?" Leeann couldn't keep the words to herself. She and Traci had come three thousand miles to hear her father was a derelict, a vagrant?

"This can't be true." Leeann stood and faced him. "My father put on a tie and jacket and went to church with his family. He rescued animals and made pizza dough from scratch. Philip, are you sure about all this?"

Traci reached out to her friend. "Calm down Leeann, let him finish."

Philip's voice got soft. "I'm trying to prepare you properly."

"Duly prepared. Where is he?"

"You are looking at him."

Leeann stared into Philip's face.

"No, straight ahead," Phillip said, pointing. "That man stretched out on the ground, fifty yards in front of us under the tree. That man is your father."

Traci put her fist to her mouth.

Leeann fixed her eyes on the figure in the distance and gasped.

"Come," Philip said, standing up.

The three of them walked across the park toward Richard Bright. Philip walked quickly and deliberately, a man on a mission. Leeann and Traci hurried to keep up.

The three knelt on the grass. "Rich, I've got some people who want to see you." At the first good look at her father, Leeann shuddered. There he was, within arm's reach, out from obscurity, as real as daylight. After all these years, she thought, we meet, and you're an old, sick, drunk man. She found it extraordinary that she felt no anger at that moment, no trepidation.

Richard's red hair was streaked gray, his once robust skin, coarse. His eyes looked like two blue sunken holes. Leeann noticed the baggy pants and black tee shirt with the words Golden Gate Bridge across it. She couldn't miss his crepe rubber sole orange grizzly boots. They were held together with broken shoelaces and comically out of place on a warm day in May. Among all the ways she envisioned finding her father, impaired was not one of them. Richard sat up and greeted them through sleepy eyes.

Philip put his hand on Richard's knee. "Your daughter Leeann has come to see you. And her friend Traci."

Richard's blank expression shifted into one of seismic shock. His eyes became large. He stared at Leeann as if reaching for some distant memory. He groped for her collar and held onto it. "Leeann, Leeann, Leeann," he said. His words were raspy and measured.

"It's been a long time." Her words carried strength and confidence. She felt the power she had given her father float away. She no longer felt like a confused child but a twenty-seven-year-old woman with clear vision, indignant her father had burdened her with his crime for half her life.

Leeann leaned back, releasing her father's grip on her collar. "You finally came to see me."

"And you remember Traci, Norm Stylofski's daughter," Leeann said, looking her way and wishing Traci didn't have that bewildered look on her face.

"My god," he said.

"You were young," Richard began in a mumble. He dropped his chin to his chest and closed his eyes. He looked up again and in garbled words said, "How is Helene?"

"Mom died when I was seventeen. Cancer. We can talk more about that later."

Richard covered his face with his hand. A long silence elapsed.

"Philip and I...Philip and I will cook...you dinner." Richard put his hand over his mouth and yawned. "Did you meet Philip? He looks out for me, but he's also a pain in my butt."

"Keep it polite, Rich."

"I remember, you know...we made that tree...and I had a motorcycle...gone...and there was a driveway..." Phrases dribbled out.

Traci picked at a blade of grass.

"Dinner," Richard mumbled again, looking at Philip. "I'll cook something...what am I saying...a feast, that's it."

"No feast tonight, Rich," Philip said.

"He thinks he...he thinks he runs the show." Richard spit out the words.

"Someone's got to," Philip said.

"You live in...I lost track...where do you live?" Richard asked Leeann.

"In Concord, Massachusetts, outside Boston." The smell of approaching rain encircled them.

"Work?"

"I'm an accountant, but I'm thinking of buying a nursery." At that, Traci jerked her head in Leeann's direction and stared.

"Your mother." He drew his knapsack closer to him, and Leeann wondered what constituted his prized possessions inside it.

"Yes, Mom owned a nursery."

"We saw your paintings in your gallery yesterday," Traci said, and all eyes turned to her.

"Waste of time," Richard grumbled. "These fingers… crippled with…" He held dirty hands in the air. His fingers were gnarled and his nails were caked with mud.

"Your ocean scenes were good," Leeann added.

Richard Bright closed his eyes and rubbed his face. "I'm tired today."

The three traded glances. Leeann wondered if her father was falling asleep or reeling from the shock of the visit.

"What's the term?" He opened his eyes wide. "Out of body experience."

Leeann knew what he meant. She felt that same out of body thing.

Richard grimaced, placing one quivering hand on his forehead. "I'm…sorry, Leeann." He closed his eyes and wiped his lower lip. "I thought you'd be better off…"

"Traci cleared her throat and spoke with authority. "Richard, do you remember the Mechanics Garage fire in 1983?"

Richard looked above her head to some distant spot in the park. "Awful."

"My dad was killed in that fire. Do you know who started it and why?"

Richard stared at Traci as if he couldn't understand what she was asking. "Norm," Richard said. He rested his chin against his chest.

"Can you tell me anything?" Traci's voice was urgent.

"Tragedy," Richard said, slurring the words. His gaze shifted to his daughter and he caught her eyes. "I can't remember…"

A rolling rumble and then a crescendo of thunder exploded over the park. The sky darkened, releasing huge drops of rain. Pigeons scattered. Wind blew. Tree limbs swayed. Lightning flashed.

"We'd better run," Philip said, getting up. Leeann and Traci stood as well.

"You go," Richard insisted, slicing his hand through the air. The rain fell harder, through spaces between leaves and branches overhead. People in the park ran for cover.

"Come on Rich, get up," Philip said.

"You go," Richard shouted over the sound of rain and claps of thunder.

"We'll get you into the car," Philip yelled.

Richard stood up, picked up his knapsack, and let Leeann and Philip help him walk across the park. Rain pelted their heads and ran down their faces. Strands of Richard's wet, disheveled hair flapped at his face. Newspaper pages swept across the grass and caught in Traci's legs. She stepped over them and ran faster. A trash barrel tipped over and papers blew out. Cars honked. Leeann tossed Traci the keys to the rental car, and Traci sprinted toward it. Rain pelted the ground, wasting no time turning it into a muddy, slippery mess. Richard, in his waterproof grizzly boots, was the only one whose feet weren't getting mud soaked.

Philip and Leeann arranged Richard on the passenger seat of Philip's Jeep, lifting first his left leg, then his right.

"This is how his life goes, good for a while, then bad for months," Philip said.

"What happens to him now?" Leeann asked.

"Rehab hasn't worked."

"You've tried hard."

Traci pulled up beside Philip's jeep and honked. Leeann looked from her father to Traci and held up her hand. "Give me a minute," she called out.

Traci nodded. She backed up and parked behind Philip's jeep.

Leeann wiped her eyes and stared at her father. "Richard," she shouted through the open window, "why did you leave us?" Leeann widened her stance. "Why? You didn't have to," she said, more loudly. Richard turned away. He squeezed his eyes shut and put down his head. Her voice boomed above the pounding rain. "Tell me right now." She pounded a closed fist on the roof of the Jeep. "Why did you leave? I wasn't going to tell." Leeann looked at Philip, then back at her father. "You screwed up my fuckin' life."

"This isn't the time." Phillip started to pull Leeann away from the car.

"I'm not done." She leaned into the passenger window, her face inches away from her father's. "I came a long way to tell you this, Richard." She clenched her fists. "I'm not going to keep your secret any longer." Tears sprang from her eyes.

Richard looked up, his eyes unfocused, his head swaying.

"I'm going to tell. When the time is right for me, I'm going to tell." She turned toward the park, empty now, the street filling with water.

Philip handed Leeann a business card. "Come to my house tomorrow morning and talk to your father. I'll keep him with me tonight." He wiped his face. "I'm sorry for you and your friend," he added. He shook his head. "If it matters, I could see there was happiness inside your dad. He couldn't take his eyes off you."

CHAPTER 33

CALIFORNIA, San Francisco and Sunset District
1998

"I'm shaking from that fiasco," Traci said, almost running a red light. At the hotel, she and Leeann turned over their car to a parking valet. Leeann walked ahead along a red carpet and stopped in the atrium in front of the hotel's signature waterfall. A thought formed in her mind, an enlightenment, which she could hold on to, which she would keep to herself: witnessing her father's suffering had the strange effect of lightening her own. Had she met a successful, wealthy, healthy, accomplished Richard Bright, with a loving wife, devoted daughters, a cherished son, her feeling of rejection by her father would have been far greater than what she felt already. Still, like Traci, she was shaken.

"Is there a bar in this joint?"

"Follow me." Traci led the way to the Slanted Door.

"Hmmm, how fitting. I feel quite slanted myself right now." They sat side by side at the empty bar.

"You were friendlier to your dad than I expected."

"Let me get one drink down before we hash over today." She ordered an apple martini. Traci scanned the listing of beer choices and opted for a Belgian beer.

Three sips in, Leeann began, "That was one un-bleep-in'-believable morning that I did not see coming."

"Go figure," Traci said.

"I kept trying to grasp the reality that I'm in the presence of my father again. Who knew that would ever happen? And when I got him to Philip's car, I told him off for walking out on my mom and me. I'm sure he was too drunk to care."

"I was too shell-shocked to say much although I did get some questions in. They went nowhere. And timing wasn't right to produce the infamous anonymous note," Traci added.

"Shell-shocked doesn't begin to describe the look on his face when he saw us."

"Sure as hell doesn't."

"He looked like an old, decrepit man," Leeann said.

"You look just like him. The dark red hair, the ice blue eyes."

"Don't forget the protruding chin. Thank you very much, Richard."

"Why do you call him Richard and not Dad?"

"He's hardly Dad." Leeann ordered a second round. "What did you think of Philip?"

"He was okay." Traci shrugged.

"I found him smug, like he was in control of Richard. Telling me not to talk to *my* father because he wasn't in the frame of mind to hear me. Fuck him." Leeann spilled her drink as she was about to take a sip, and vodka dribbled down her chin.

"You jealous of Philip?"

"Jealous? Screw you, too." A third round appeared.

"Hey, what's this about you buying a nursery?"

"I'm toying with the idea. Could just be a pipe dream." After a sip, Leeann said, "I kinda lost it with my father at the end there. It felt damn good."

Traci looked down at her beer. "Yeah, you were screaming. I heard you say, 'I wasn't going to tell.' "

"You did?" Leeann gripped her glass with both hands.

"Yeah, you were loud."

"Hmm, I remember telling him he was emotionally abusive to Mom and me, but I never told anyone that."

"Because?"

"Because we were a family and I thought he was a good dad even though he had these rages."

"You said all that to him today?" The sound of ice being crushed drew their attention to the bartender making a frozen drink.

"No, I'm telling *you*. I'm explaining why I said, 'I never told anyone.' "

"For the record, your exact words were, 'I wasn't going to tell.' You hiding something, Leeann?" Traci's eyes were narrow slits.

"I'm hiding nothing. Drink up. I want to get out of these wet clothes. Shit, you can be a pain in the ass."

"You, too."

"And for the record, we're going to Philip's tomorrow morning for breakfast. My dad will be there. We can ask questions."

"Fine with me." Traci left several dollar bills on the counter. They headed for the lobby in search of the elevator.

Leeann felt relieved and conflicted all at once. She was free to tell the secret, if she was ready to let it go. Coming to San Francisco had been a good move for her.

They arrived at Philip's house in the Sunset District at nine o'clock Sunday morning. Philip opened the door, dropping his eyes to the floor. "I'm sorry," he said. "When I got up this morning to check on Richard, the sofa was empty, and he was gone." Philip was breathing hard and didn't look as put together as he had the previous two days. Gone was the formal white shirt. Today he was in a polo shirt and jeans. "Your father couldn't face you. The past eats away at him."

"Don't worry, Leeann and I are thick-skinned. It's not as if we were invited to California."

"I don't know if I'm relieved or disappointed," Leeann said. She and Traci accepted Philip's invitation to join him for breakfast in his dining room where shades filtered bright light. He put out three plates and silverware. In the middle of the table he placed a pitcher of coffee. Philip served hard-boiled eggs and orange juice and small biscuits with jam. They discussed their jobs and Philip's business. They talked about Massachusetts and California. There was no talk about Richard until they'd nearly finished eating.

"When Richard is sober, he's intelligent and funny," Philip said.

"How does he keep his painting business going?" Leeann asked.

210

"It's difficult. He starts a sketch of an automobile…"

Traci spoke up. "And you finish painting it so it can be sold. I saw the paint on your hands and forearms on Friday. Framers don't have paint all over their arms."

Philip lowered his head. "I know it's wrong, but I keep thinking that he'll be well soon. I don't want him to lose his business. Yes, I do complete his paintings."

Philip was growing on Leeann. She found him more likable. He ran his own business, looked out for people, and broke rules when he found it necessary. And it occurred to her that Philip, in his forties, was a constant guide and helper to Richard. They were more than landlord and tenant.

"Thank you for making the effort to come here," Philip said. He left the room and returned with something in his hand. He pressed a photo into Leeann's palm, a picture of eight-year-old Leeann and Richard on a sled on a snowy, steep hill. Leeann was in front, tucked into her father's arms, which were wrapped around her in an embrace. Ski hats and scarves covered part of their faces, but not their wide grins.

Leeann looked at it briefly, thanked Philip, and handed the photo to Traci, who looked at it and said, "Cool." It wasn't cool. It was as painful a photograph as Leeann had ever seen. She would never take a second look. There were tears at the edges of her eyes. She fought to keep control of her emotions, but it was not possible.

Philip walked Traci and Leeann to their car. He put his arms around both of them. "Maybe in six months, you'll come back. Things will be different."

"We'll stay in touch," Traci said.

That night, in the room they shared, Traci asked Leeann to turn down the volume to the television. She wanted to replay a message her sister had left on their hotel room voice mail: *"Hi Trace, just got word. Detective John Handley has suffered from Alzheimer's for the past five years. He did not write the anonymous note. Keep searching. How did your day go?"*

CHAPTER 34

WESTERN MASSACHUSETTS, Berkshire Ridge
May and June, 1988
Leeann Bright, 17 years old

Helene Bright's ashes fluttered in the wind, settling on the choppy waters of the Piscataqua River. Leeann stood straight, arms across her chest as John Wicker released her mother's ashes back to nature. Mike Holly recited a prayer. Maddie Holly took Leeann's hand and read Helene's favorite poem by Maya Angelou. "The free bird leaps on the back of the wind and floats downstream." Leeann barely heard the words. She was mesmerized, numbed by the specks of her mother's ashes being carried out to sea.

The ride home was silent. Mike and Maddie sat in the front seat. John Wicker, sitting in the back next to Leeann, stared out the window. Leeann sat slumped next to him, fighting back tears. She hadn't thought of bringing flowers to the ceremony to honor her mother.

That same day, Leeann moved into the Holly's upstairs spare bedroom. Maddie apologized for the old wicker furniture. "It will feel more like home when Mike brings over your desk later this week."

"Not a problem." Leeann sat on the bed, eyeing a collection of books on a shelf, looking forward to some time alone.

Maddie lingered. "Do you like the yellow curtains?"

"They're nice. They remind me of daffodils and marigolds." She decided she would read the book on Medieval China, a place far from Berkshire Ridge and her reality.

Maddie backed out of the room and closed the door. No longer interested in reading, Leeann lay back, remembering the morning, the prayers and poems, and watching her mother's ashes scatter on the waves, watching life as she knew it and her mother float away.

After dinner, the four of them—Maddie, Mike, their son Patrick and Leeann—sat on the screened-in porch and ate Maddie's homemade peach shortcake. Mike lit a cigar. Patrick and Leeann played Monopoly on the floor.

About ten o'clock, Maddie went into the house and called for Leeann to join her upstairs. She was in Patrick's room rummaging through an oversized cedar chest. The room was dark except for some light from the hallway. Maddie offered her a white blanket.

"You'll want to keep this spread at the foot of your bed."

Leeann brushed Maddie's fingers as she took the blanket. She apologized and realized how lame an apology sounded for touching her coach's hand.

"I've been thinking about your mother, Leeann." She stopped and sat down on the bed. "She loved you very much." She cleared her throat. "In the hospital, she told me many times how much you had done for her—all the housework, the chores, the bills, the calls you made for her. 'All that and then there was her homework and school and softball,' she used to say. 'The best years, when Leeann should be hanging out with friends, but she never once complained.' She was so proud of you when you got your scholarship." Maddie turned her head as if to get a better look at Leeann.

"I was proud of her, too," Leeann said, not wanting to hear this, not wanting to think about those last months.

"I want you to know it's going to hurt for a while. A long while."

Leeann grew queasy, afraid she would break down in sobs. She wondered why the room was dark but grateful the shadows hid the tears welling in her eyes.

"Maddie?" Leeann looked at her feet.

"Yes?"

"Thank you," she said, a lump in her throat, "for everything."

Leeann spent the next day wandering around her new home, moving from room to room, from the porch to the end of the driveway, crisscrossing the immense front lawn and back to the porch where she sat, bored and restless, wondering what the Holly's expected of her. Could she help herself to a glass of milk from the refrigerator? Was it okay to snack after dinner? Could she put her feet on the coffee table while watching television? It wasn't clear to her how to be the perfect guest. She yearned to return to her house, hang out in her old room, sit on the shaky kitchen chairs and rub her hands across the oak table. There she knew the rules. By afternoon, the pain that had been hammering her shoulder ran up her neck and settled in front of her head. She went to her room and eased into the wicker chair. She would never feel normal again.

On Saturday, Leeann stopped by the nursery to pick up her paycheck. John, now the owner of the nursery, put down a box of multi-colored impatiens and gave Leeann an exuberant pat on the back.

"I'm giving my notice," she said. "I can't be here."

The corners of John's mouth turned down. "We're going to miss you."

"Coach Maddie's hiring me as assistant softball coach for the summer."

"If you change your mind, you're always free to come back." John handed Leeann her check along with a cardboard box filled with sympathy cards. "They're from customers all over New England. Your mother was loved by people in Berkshire Ridge and beyond," John said. "These letters say how much pleasure they got from her nursery. They appreciated how much work she put into keeping the business running, even when she was ill."

It would be a while before Leeann could bring herself to read them.

"How are you doing at Maddie's house?"

Leeann shrugged and said, "Fine."

"Everything okay there?" He tilted his head.

"It's fine."

"Good. You be sure to drop by once in a while and say hello."

Leeann left through the door leading to the south parking lot and past the cashier's shed. She bumped into Traci carrying a bag of potting soil over her shoulder.

"What are you doing here?" She'd seen little of Traci during their final semester of high school. They'd played softball together but hadn't hung out much.

"I work here."

Traci working at her mother's nursery? Unbelievable! She didn't know a geranium from a dandelion. But it was John Wicker's nursery now.

"Why here?"

"John's the Rotary Club president. The club and a bunch of guys who worked at Mechanics Garage raised money for me. I'm going to Atlantic Community College, right down the street from where you're going. I'm working here for extra money." Traci's back was facing the shed and she didn't see the line forming at the register. Leeann motioned to her that customers needed her.

"I'll see you in Boston," Leeann said. "Let's not lose touch."

"We'll both be so busy with classes."

"No, really, Traci, I'll make sure we see each other in Boston."

"And I'll see you at graduation next week, huh?" Traci called out to Leeann.

"Not going to graduation. Don't like the hype."

Maddie and Mike insisted Leeann attend graduation. It was a milestone marking her achievements in academics and sports despite enormous obstacles. She should be there to soak up the glory. Mike put on a tie and jacket. Maddie wore a pale pink dress she'd made and carried a matching pink purse. Leeann stood tall in her red gown. On the second Sunday in June, under a sapphire sky, they sat on the football field among hundreds of students, parents, and friends for a ceremony full of pomp and circumstance. The high school principal, Mr. Hurd, reminded graduates to be true to themselves. The valedictorian was Sammy Smith, with whom Leeann had flirted all through senior year. She'd always hoped he would ask her out—he never did—but then again, she was not in a position to date with all she had to do at home. He spoke about gratitude.

Under normal circumstances, the day would have left Leeann feeling pumped. She was heading to Boston University with a four-year scholarship a few days before Labor Day to live in a high-rise dorm with its view of the Boston skyline. She walked onto the stage to the cheers of her softball teammates. She should have had a glow on her face. The principal handed her a diploma, that piece of parchment releasing her from childhood, launching her into adulthood, but all she thought of was her mother, who had wanted to live long enough to witness this day. Mr. Hurd shook Leeann's hand, but held onto it longer than he did the other students' even when Leeann turned to walk away.

CHAPTER 35

WESTERN MASSACHUSETTS, Berkshire Ridge
July, 1988
Leeann Bright, 17 years old

Leeann's planned trip from Berkshire Ridge to the New Hampshire coast would take two hours. Having gotten permission to use Maddie's car, she got on the Massachusetts Turnpike and headed east. An hour in, traffic came to a halt. She could see the Flower Mart from the highway and watched customers come and go from the largest wholesale nursery in the state. An ambulance pulled around her and squeezed through one line of cars to get to the accident scene. Traffic started to move after a flatbed truck removed a mangled Chevy Blazer. Leeann got off the highway and headed to the Flower Mart. She purchased four-dozen Blue Iris and headed to Portsmouth, New Hampshire.

She parked in the lot of a motel at the start of the bridge that spanned the Piscataqua River. Carrying the massive blue bouquet, she walked the narrow sidewalk to the bridge's peak, aware of the cars whizzing by her. There she stood peering over the railing at the river, gray-blue and flat as a canyon wall. Her mind wandered back to her mother, and those thoughts gave her comfort. She recalled the days of their working together at the nursery and the afternoons eating hot fudge sundaes on Mel's porch. A flashing blue light interrupted her memories. A police cruiser stopped on the bridge, and a New Hampshire state trooper stepped out. "Are you all right?" he asked.

"Yes, fine."

"We got a call that you've been standing here for a very long time."

"My mother is down below. Her ashes, I mean."

"Too dangerous to stand here, miss. Please move along."

Leeann took a step closer to the railing, lifted the four-dozen Blue Iris and tossed them upward and outward. She watched them sail from the sky downward and land in the river. "I'm done."

The trooper waited on the bridge, as Leeann turned, and with her arms swinging at her side, hurried along the sidewalk. Once inside Maddie's car, she paused for a moment, talking to her mother. "Now you have your flowers, Mom. I love you. Rest in peace." She started the car, merged into the traveling lane and took the first exit west toward Massachusetts.

.

CHAPTER 36

EASTERN MASSACHUSETTS, Boston and surrounding suburbs
1998

The Boston-bound plane touched down at Logan Airport at midnight, and Traci released her grip on the arms of her seat. "I'm sorry it turned out this way, Leeann. I won't forget you did this for me."

"I did it for me too, and I don't regret it."

"We didn't accomplish anything."

"Not true. I know how my father's life turned out," Leeann said. "I got an ending to my story. But can you believe my father dumped me a second time? Can you fuckin' believe that?"

"Not for nothin' but I wouldn't have shown up to face you at Philip's house either. He's pretty much of a mess emotionally, huh?" Traci folded her arms across her chest.

"You giving up your investigation?" Leeann asked.

"Not a chance. On Saturday I'm going to Berkshire Ridge and talking to some of the guys who fought the fire."

She looked at Leeann out of the corner of her eye. "I'd like you with me."

"I'm sure they won't remember a thing," Leeann said. "But, if you want me, I'll be there."

At baggage claim, Traci declined Leeann's invitation to stay with her that night.

"Come on, you don't need that long ride home at this hour."

"Thanks, but it's time I get back to my house."

It was good to lie in her bed again, although Leeann couldn't fall asleep. She couldn't shake the image of her father, drunk with bloodshot eyes, sitting beneath a tree in a park in his ghastly orange boots. She was proud of the way she stood up to him and spoke the words over and over in her head: *Richard, I'm not going to keep your secret any longer.* She thought of her mother and John Wicker, the likely author of the anonymous note, she guessed. Leeann got out of bed and went downstairs. In a file cabinet, she searched for the last communication from John Wicker, a letter he sent her six years before when she landed her first job after college. If John were the author, the handwriting would match. But Leeann could find no letter. She turned on her computer. She was in awe of this new world-wide-web and was getting used to doing searches of all types. Maybe John was still in Florida running his landscaping business. In the browser window, she typed "John Wicker + Tampa, Florida + landscaping." Her search pulled up a page with a series of links. The muscles in her throat tightened when she read: *John Wicker Obituary.* Leeann opened the link and read: *John Steven Wicker, 52, of*

Tampa, formerly of Berkshire Ridge, Massachusetts, died after a lengthy illness with his family by his side. He leaves his wife Jocelyn Wicker and a brother Ryan Wicker from Chicago. A memorial service will be held on Saturday, June 9, 10:00 a.m. at Congregational Church in Tampa. Donations may be made to the American Lymphoma and Leukemia Society.

Leeann lay awake for hours. A burning behind her eyes wouldn't go away. She didn't think about her father or Karen Downey or her appointment the next morning with Attorney Sumner Smith. She thought about John Wicker, the kind man who washed her face the night she fell off her bike after being chased in an alley by Roland Barnes. She could see now that John and her mother had been in love. Leeann went to the kitchen for some orange juice to soothe her dry throat. She sat drinking out of the carton. According to the obituary, John Wicker died two years earlier. He did not write the anonymous note.

CHAPTER 37

EASTERN MASSACHUSETTS, Boston and surrounding suburbs
1998

Attorney Sumner Smith guided Leeann into a conference room. He carried a bent legal pad with one remaining blank crumpled page left on it. He didn't carry a file or the papers Leeann faxed to him the week before. This was the legal genius Ben raved about?

Sunlight reflected off a massive mahogany table, and Leeann folded her hands on its surface. Sumner tried but failed to stifle a yawn. "Stayed up way too late last night reading," he said. "Got to stop that but I love stories." He wrote something on the yellow-lined paper, a date maybe. "The answers to all the concerns of human existence lie in literature. Are you a reader, Leeann?"

"Some." Leeann made a mental note to shake this guy and find an attorney who got right down to business as she did with her clients.

"What was the last book you read?" His voice was gravelly-deep.

"Soil Samples and Landscaping Solutions," Leeann answered, staring straight past Sumner to the window offering an ocean view.

"A spell binder, huh?"

"I'm a gardener." She offered a weak smile.

"Do you have a good book recommendation?"

Humor the man, Leeann thought, he *is* Ben's boss. "Well, I suppose it never hurts to start with Mr. William Shakespeare."

"Shakespeare. Okay, good one." Leeann pulled her copies of legal documents from her briefcase and placed them on the conference table.

"You're getting impatient," Sumner said. "I wanted to get to know you a little before we begin. Ben has talked about you for quite some time."

"Don't believe a word of it."

Sumner threw back his head and laughed. "No, all good stuff." He looked at his watch then at Leeann. "I can't act as your attorney."

"Did I do something wrong?"

"I can't represent you because you don't need an attorney." Leeann lifted her head. "Eric Downy recanted his story. Seems his memory has come into focus. He remembers now that you did *not* crash your car into him. He blames himself for the accident. There is no lawsuit."

Leeann gripped the corner of the conference table. "It's over?"

Sumner stood and reached for her hand. Leeann stood and staggered backward before banging into a chair. "Thank you, Sumner, thank you."

"Nothing to thank me for. It was a strange case from the start." He made a sweeping gesture. "Go enjoy your life. And do not contact Karen or Eric Downey. Period."

"No, certainly not."

"Ben wants you to call him. He's in Yarmouth." Sumner walked her to an empty cubicle where she dialed his number.

"Sumner told me the good news this morning," Ben said.

"I feel as if the Himalayas have been lifted from my shoulders. Thank you, Ben."

"Sorry things didn't work out in San Francisco, Leeann. I talked to Traci yesterday."

"Yeah, dismal trip in some ways." She tucked her brief-case under her arm.

"I've got to go. I'm late for work." Standing at the eleva-tor, on the fortieth floor, she vowed to put her father and the trip to California out of her mind. She had too many things in life to be happy about, to be grateful for. She cut through Myrtle Park on Congress Street where the air expanded with a generous scent of fresh earth. Leeann thought about Eric Downey, his temper, the scar on his chin, his earring, and his crazy-ass mother. Eric Downey, who rode his bike in the rain, fished for trout, threw them back in the river, cut classes, and told the truth when it mattered.

CHAPTER 38

MASSACHUSETTS, Berkshire Ridge
1998

Leeann pushed aside a plate of baked ziti and watched Traci savage an order of fried calamari.

"Come on, eat up," Traci urged.

"Lost my appetite."

Traci stopped eating. "Nervous about this afternoon?"

"I guess."

The two friends sat in a booth at Loden's Grill for lunch before interviewing two Berkshire Ridge firefighters, Ted Janis and Peter Holmes.

Traci was reassuring. "They're eager to talk. Ted remembers Roland Barnes well. Called him 'charming as a Python.' " She sat back and patted her stomach. "God I ate too much."

"You're a good friend, Traci." Her voice got lost in the clatter of dishes being piled onto a tray beside them.

"Where did that come from?"

Leeann raised her shoulders and lowered them. "I think you're a great person."

"What have you been smoking?"

"Funny." Leeann paid the bill and they left through the back door. Outside, beyond Loden's property was a rolling meadow where Leeann and Traci shared countless bike rides as twelve year olds the spring and summer of 1983. By that November they were inseparable.

"Pretty sight this time of year," Traci said, pointing to horses grazing.

But all Leeann could see was the body of Traci's father amid charred debris. She saw firefighters, their faces shattered when they discovered him in the early hours of daylight, and pallbearers carrying Norm Stylofski's casket into St. Mary's Church.

She shook away the vision. "It's hot, let's go." Leeann said. "I'm taking us to the old softball field."

"We left air-conditioned Loden's Grill to bake in a hot ballpark?"

"Yes."

At one o'clock, they leaned over the chain link fence surrounding Waters Field. Crumpled paper cups and empty soda bottles littered the grass. A recent string of hot, dry days had wilted the overgrown weeds. The once green outfield was now covered with grass the color of ivory.

"Ya kind of feel as if we should go out there and clean it up," Leeann said, under her breath.

Traci suggested they pay a visit to their former coach, Maddie Holly. "Maybe even take her to dinner tonight."

"Not interested," Leeann said. "Things didn't end well with Maddie and me. Her son was a major problem."

"You couldn't get along with a ten-year-old?"

Patrick was not happy I was getting his mother's attention."

"How do you know that?"

"He started stealing from me. Clothes, money, books. I confronted him and he literally told me to get the fuck out of his house. So, in the middle of July, weeks before I was planning to leave for B.U., I bought an Amtrak ticket to Boston and said farewell. Maddie was pissed I didn't finish out the season helping her coach but I couldn't tell her why I was leaving. I lied and said my dorm was ready for me and I wanted to settle in early."

"Damn shame," Traci said. "Softball kept me out of trouble for sure. Maddie saved my life with all the attention and encouragement she gave me."

"Nice."

"No one ever said I was good at anything except her."

Little League players carrying bats and gloves gathered onto the field. Leeann suggested they sit in the bleachers, and Traci followed. They climbed to the highest bench overlooking the field.

"You know," Leeann began, "the day my dad took off for good, everything turned upside down. Like it did for you when you lost your dad. I didn't know how to handle things. I made mistakes." The inside of her mouth cracked from dryness. She squeezed her fists open and closed. She stood up and lost her balance. Traci reached out to her.

"I know who set fire to Mechanics Garage, Traci. I know who killed your dad." Blood rushed to her cheeks and ears and eyes. She forced a breath. A look of confusion crossed Traci's face. Leeann closed her eyes and whispered, "It was my father." She thought the words would cut off her breathing. After a long silence, words she'd bottled up for years tumbled out. "I saw him running from the Garage as it burned. He told me the fire was an accident. He made me promise I would never tell *anyone*." When I got older, I realized he had set the fire." She turned to Traci. "Kids do things for their parents. It wasn't right. There was no justice for your family because of me." Traci was staring at the ground, shaking her head. Leeann's limbs trembled. "I'm sorry, Traci. I wouldn't blame you for never speaking to me again."

Traci lifted her head. "Damn it, Leeann, I've looked up to you my whole life." Her face was bright with sweat, her shirt drenched. "You just kicked me in the gut."

Leeann sat down. "I can't stop telling you how sorry I am."

"Your dad was a prick to have put that burden on you."

"Traci, he did not know your dad was in the building that night. I know that."

"Tell me what you saw. Every detail."

"I'll tell you everything, but you've got to take a ride with me first."

Traci sat in the passenger seat, mumbling, "What a nightmare. How could you have kept this from me? What a friggin' nightmare this is."

Leeann exhaled deep breaths, her head spinning, a part of her in shock over what she had just done. She drove to the center of town and parked in front of War Memorial Park opposite the Fire Department and Police Station. She led the way across the street. Traci traipsed behind.

"Where the hell...?"

"Just come," Leeann said.

They climbed the steps of the Berkshire Ridge Police Station and entered the lobby. Through a pane of glass, Leeann asked the officer if she could talk to the detective on duty.

"I'm here to report a crime," she said. "Arson. I was a witness."

In a closet-size, airless room, Leeann and Traci and Detective Jerry Stearns, a chubby man with sagging jowls, sat around a wobbly table.

"I remember the fire well. It was in 1983. I'd just moved to town." Detective Stearns questioned Leeann for an hour, tape recording her statements and recollections about her father and mother, and what happened the night of the fire and in the days that followed. He sat expressionless, listening as she described her memories of that evening.

As she finished, she looked at Traci and then to the white-haired detective. "I couldn't feel worse if I'd killed Mr. Stylofski myself."

"You were a traumatized kid," the detective said, his first hint of compassion filling the room. "Leeann, you are not in any jeopardy."

Leeann looked at the floor after accepting a handkerchief from Detective Stearns. Damn these tears. They were flowing hard down her face, saturating her skin, dripping into her mouth. Through blurred eyes, Leeann apologized to the detective and, over and over again, to Traci, who reached out and put her hand on Leeann's arm.

"There's more." Leeann took a sip of water from a paper cup the detective had given her when they first sat down.

"My father lives in California. I have a contact who can reach him if you want to arrest him."

The detective arched an eyebrow. "Roland Barnes died about ten years ago—he'd always been real deep in debt. He likely paid your father to set that fire. The police concluded long ago that insurance fraud was at the root of the crime."

"What's going to happen to Richard?" Traci asked.

"Lacking a confession, with the statute of limitations and not much evidence other than Leeann's words, it may be impossible to put together a case strong enough to convict. But that's not up to me."

Traci chipped away at the grass covering her father's marker at Berkshire Ridge Cemetery. Leeann wandered close by, reading headstones, looking for old dates and unusual names, and when she found some, she'd call them out to Traci. For the first time in fifteen years, Leeann had nothing to hide. Her lie, her secret, or rather her father, had no hold on her any longer. She waited for a feeling of lightness but it didn't come. She expected joy but felt only sadness for Traci's pain. The sight of so many graves drew the breath out of her. She sat next to Traci and read Norm Stylofski's marker, clean now, his name and birthdate visible.

Traci spoke in a whisper. "After my dad died, I experienced something I'd never known before. Peace in my house." Leeann turned in Traci's direction. "My parents fought every day of my life. Rotten thing to do to kids. My dad was a wicked drunk, but maybe if he'd lived, he would have reformed himself. I'll never know."

"That must be hard to accept, the never knowing."

They walked around the cemetery without speaking as if wanting to hold onto the day. When the afternoon light faded, they headed through the gates of the cemetery toward Leeann's car. "Let's drive through the old neighborhood," Traci said. Leeann grimaced. "Are you sure?"

"I'm sure." They drove to Summit Avenue to Leeann's old house, the cape with its purple rhododendrons in full bloom, but didn't get out of the car. Leeann recalled herself standing in her yard at twelve years old on the day her father left home. There were tipped over trash barrels, the broken mailbox and rickety fence. She saw herself looking out the living room window through dirty panes of glass as her father backed his truck down the driveway, waving his arm at her. There was another scene she'd imagined hundreds of times. He stopped his truck and opened the passenger door to let her climb inside. She rushed from the house to the passenger side door. But today she didn't climb in. She slammed the door shut and watched as the truck sped off, tires digging into the gravel along the driveway, and vanished.

CHAPTER 39

MASSACHUSETTS, Berkshire Ridge and Cape Cod
1998

Traci leaned against the ice machine outside the town's donut shop, satisfying her urge to eat three freshly made jelly donuts.

Leeann was on her cell phone. "Hey Josh, new development here on the Mechanics Garage arson story." Her voice cracked as she spoke. Traci, alternately wiped jelly and sugar off her face and guzzled coffee. "I'll do one interview for you and the *Advocate* but it's got to be right now. I'm ready to talk."

"Shit. I'm mowing my in-law's lawn."

"You'll want this story, Josh. Witness comes clean after fifteen years."

Traci canceled the interviews with both firefighters and told them there was no need to reschedule. Traci and Leeann waited for Josh in the *Advocate's* parking lot, near an empty space with a sign, *Reserved for Editor*. Josh showed up in beat-up sneakers, shorts and a worn tee shirt. Safety glasses hung around his neck. He tracked wet grass shavings through the newsroom, which looked tired and in need of paint. Leeann and Traci traipsed behind. Reporters at their computers looked up and exchanged glances. Leeann put down her head.

"I can't get ahead of the police," Josh said, sitting at his desk, the door to his office closed, his phone turned off. "I can't name a suspect, if that's what you're about to do. I can only write what Leeann says she saw, and the fact that she's come forward."

Award plaques covered one wall in Josh's office. Bookshelves bulged with newspapers and journals. Josh popped a Lifesaver into his mouth and turned on his computer. He moved with an eagerness of a man who loved his job. Traci propped her feet on the coffee table and clasped her hands behind her head. "The story's going to be about you too, your role in pursuing a cold case," Josh said, pointing to Traci.

"Be absolutely sure you write this: victim's daughter Traci Patricia Stylofski is on the brink of proving her father did not set the Mechanics Garage fire. Here's your headline: *Has the Mechanics Garage arson fire been solved? Victim's daughter responsible for chain of events that brought witness forward.*"

"Mind if I write my own story?" Josh said to Traci. Leeann knew Traci didn't take the comment as a dig, even if Josh hadn't flashed a half-grin. He placed a cassette tape recorder in front of Leeann. His skinny fingers manipulated the machine, and it occurred to Leeann, ever so briefly, that Josh had beaten leukemia twice. Traci stood up and paced. "You'd better get every word of what she's about to say. It's one un-fuckin'-believable story." Leeann clasped both hands on the sides of her face and squeezed as if she were keeping her head from exploding. A boulder-sized knot formed in her stomach.

"Tell me why, after all these years, you're coming forward." Josh asked.

Leeann lifted one hand off her face. With her thumb, like a hitchhiker, she pointed in the direction of Traci.

Traci stayed behind at her sister's house that night. She wanted to wake early the next morning to purchase the newspaper and read Josh's exclusive story. She expected to see her photograph on page one, she'd told Leeann, who declined to be photographed. In fact, Leeann wanted to get out of town before the story broke. After the interview with Josh, she called Ben.

"I need to tell you something."

His voice jumped an octave. "Are you in trouble *again?*"

"I'm not in trouble. Can I come see you tonight?"

"Come now."

The route to Yarmouth hugged the curve of the ocean. Blackness surrounded her, except for the occasional oncoming headlight and the glow of the moon, which appeared in the sky straight ahead.

Ben was waiting for her in the screened-in front porch. It was almost eleven o'clock. He handed her a glass of wine when she opened the door. She held onto her stomach, staring at the dark through the porch screen.

"My dad killed Traci's father." Tears collected behind her eyes. As the words tumbled out, Ben's mouth dropped open and stayed open until Leeann finished her story, all of it: the fire, her father, the anonymous note, and what Leeann had confessed hours earlier in Berkshire Ridge. "He didn't mean to kill anyone and certainly not Norm, who was a friend of his. Norm went there to have his whiskey and be alone." A chill went through her body. "Traci's life changed in an instant."

Ben soothed her with words for hours more. "That you've carried this inside for years, Leeann, just crushes me." In his room, they collapsed onto the bed. He covered her with a blanket. They fell asleep. Her clothes lay in a heap on the floor beside the bed.

When she awoke, Leeann could hear Ben on the phone canceling his meetings for the day.

"I'm intruding on your job," she said to him.

"No, I want to spend the day with you. Let's get breakfast."

In the shed behind the house, Ben found two bikes for them to use. They rode along the harbor, slowing down to look at lobster boats tied to moorings. Morning fog was lifting.

"You did an incredible thing yesterday. Do you feel content, relief maybe?"

"Numb."

"You've never told one person in all these years?"

"I almost told my mother once. We were at Wexler Lake, and I chickened out. And then I saw a counselor in college. I was having a hard time with my mother's death. But after a few weeks, this counselor started pumping me about my father and I said to myself, 'Whoa, I'm out of here.' I never went back. I was afraid if I confessed my secret, she'd turn me into the police for covering up a crime."

They rode along the weather-bleached boards of the pier. Two seagulls landed on a ledge of rock that jutted into the ocean. At a dock not six feet away, an old man, sunburned and tattooed, stood hip-deep in water next to his boat and off-loaded his catch. The briny smell of fish drifted toward them. In town, they ordered breakfast at a café, called Selene's, its windows opened to the salty humidity. Leeann placed her sunglasses on the table.

"What your dad did was hideous, making his child keep a secret like that." Ben opened his menu. "You don't seem happy for the brave act you did yesterday."

"Because I've lost Traci." Leeann moved her hand across her eyes. "I saw it in her face when I left her at Vivian's last night. We had this great talk in the cemetery, but when I dropped her off, she had a look on her face that said, 'I'm done with you.' She didn't say a word, didn't hug me, just waved and closed the door."

"She was in shock," Ben insisted. He placed his hand on top of hers. "The two of you need each other."

"No, everything is changing." She closed her eyes. "A wall went up. I know Traci. Honestly, I can't blame her."

After ordering, Leeann reached into her pocket and pulled out the envelope with the anonymous note sent to Josh two months before. "I guess I can throw out this note. We'll never know who wrote it, and that will irk me forever."

Ben took the note from her and studied it. Leeann had looked it over many times for clues. "There's not much here to look at." He held the envelope up to the light and turned it over in his hand. "I don't see anything unusual." He gave it back, shaking his head.

"Oh my god," Leeann said. "I see it now. The author." She slammed her hand on the table. "It was there all the time. Look at the two stamps." Her eyes widened.

"One's a regular thirty-three cent postal stamp," Ben said.

"And the other's a decorative wildlife stamp. The postal stamp covers the cost of postage, but the other is there for show."

"For what purpose?"

"Look closely at the scene on the stamp," Leeann said. "What do you see?"

"I see a picture of a swamp, some reeds and a turtle," Ben said, squinting.

"A turtle, right. The anonymous note was written by my old pediatrician, Douglas Turtle."

"You think so?" he asked, his brow wrinkling.

"This man had toy turtles all over his office, photos of turtles on his walls, turtle stationery, turtle tie clips, turtle ties, turtle stickers. He was obsessed. God, he must be in his nineties."

"Will you call him?"

"No, I'll pay him a visit and ask him why he wrote the note and sent it to Josh." She put the note and envelope in her purse when pancakes and eggs arrived.

After breakfast, they rode to the dunes, and locked their bikes to a pole in the beach parking lot. "Today's the kite festival," Ben said. "Let's go down to the beach and watch." Sand-slippery steps led them along a twisting path up a hill with wheat-colored beach grass and salt-raggedy rosa rugosa prickling against Leeann's arms and legs. Sand oozed between her toes and sandals. At the top of the hill, where wild grass gave way to unblemished sand, Leeann froze at the sights before her: the ocean, calm and royal blue, its diamond-studded luster stretching to the horizon, and dozens of multi-colored kites swirling in the air.

"I'll race you down hill." Leeann's gold hoop earrings glistened in the sun as she took off running. At the bottom of the hill, she collapsed onto the sand, close enough to the Calypso band and kite flyers to get a good glimpse, but far enough away to not be in their way. Ben sat down beside her. If only they had more privacy, Leeann thought. She put her arm around him, and he kissed her. She didn't pull away.

"I'm buying the Silver Sword Nursery," she said. "The auction's on Friday."

"You're giving up your career? Are you serious?"

"Yes, the accounting career that's brought me to a state of total burn-out."

Ben maintained his look of skepticism.

"Besides, I'm a witness, who, for years, hid a felony of arson in a building in which a man was killed. I'm not good publicity for a CPA firm."

"You'd sell your house?"

"Of course. There's an antique colonial that's part of the property I'm buying. I'll live there and fix it up. I'd like you to be at the auction, Ben."

He nodded. "I can make it, but are you sure you want to go through with this?"

"Yes, and I want us to get back together." She grabbed his hand. "I love you very much."

He pulled her close. "I know you, Leeann. You'll be hyper-focused on getting your nursery going. I will be the last thing on your mind."

"No Ben, you're wrong. I want to love someone, namely you, and get married. I want a family. That's what's most important to me." She looked away from him, her eyes on the kites above them. "My mother would be happy knowing I'm buying a nursery."

They stayed on the beach for hours until the kite flyers and musicians and swimmers were gone, and the beach spread before them like a vacant field.

CHAPTER 40

EASTERN MASSACHUSETTS, Gloucester and Boston suburbs
1998

Leeann pulled her new yellow plaid sundress from the upstairs closet and searched for her sandals. By the end of the day, she would know why, after all this time, Dr. Turtle wrote the anonymous note to Josh and how he knew Richard Bright was involved in the Mechanics Garage fire. She hurried to shower and dress. For a split second, she imagined Dr. Turtle studying her face in disbelief, stating, "You are mistaken. I never wrote a note to Josh Wilson." She left at noon for the hour's ride to Gloucester.

The Tides Rest Home sat on a rocky embankment overlooking the coast. It was a three-story English Tudor and appeared to have borne the brunt of winds off the ocean on its north facing side. Two black shutters were ripped from their mountings and lay caked with dirt on the ground. The paint was peeling in between the wooden timbers, leaving brown weathered stains on the plastered exterior structure.

The nurse, who'd answered the phone that morning, told Leeann to follow the stone path to the rear of the building.

In the center of the back yard was a Star Magnolia tree. Its buds had sprung open weeks before, and now its saucer-shaped petals lay scattered on the grass. Dr. Douglas Turtle, wheelchair-bound, was sitting under that tree. He was a slimmer version of the doctor Leeann remembered. There were more lines around his blue eyes. His skin, loose and sagging, was almost transparent.

"I've been expecting you," he said. He was hunched over, but when he saw Leeann, he struggled to straighten up.

"Dr. Turtle." Leeann grabbed his outstretched hand. She held onto fingers that were bumpy and misshapen. Fat, purple veins crisscrossed the top of his hand.

"These ninety-five year-old fingers won't do what I want them to do anymore." He must have seen Leeann's eyes linger on his hand. "I order coffee every morning just to have something hot to wrap them around."

"You're a long way from Berkshire Ridge," Leeann said. She dragged a plastic folding chair from a few feet away and placed it next to Dr. Turtle. She sat down.

"How did you find me?" the doctor asked.

"Traci Stylofski's sister Vivian knows everything about anyone who lives or has lived in Berkshire Ridge. She told me where I'd find you."

"After my wife died," he said, pausing for a minute to catch his breath, "I moved to Gloucester to live with my brother. We both live here now." He glanced at an upper floor of the rest home. Leeann looked upward, too. Dr. Turtle wiped his dry lips with the back of his hand. Leeann waited for him to continue talking. "I'm glad you're here Leeann, because I have a question for you, but first I want to tell you how pleased I was with the article Josh Wilson wrote on Sunday in the *Berkshire Ridge Advocate*.

"I haven't read it, but I heard it got people's attention," Leeann said.

"I read it on the Internet. Josh is quite a good writer. But I was mostly proud of you, Leeann. How are you doing?" He moved his hand forward and touched her arm.

"Good. Crazy week. I'm shaken up, but I feel good." She bobbed her head up and down. "Real good."

A breeze stirred the branches of the tree overhead. The sun moved behind a cloud, sending a chill through the air. Dr. Turtle grasped for the blanket on his lap but it slipped out of his hand. Leeann stood and draped it over Dr. Turtle's chest and tucked it under his arms.

"Leeann, what day is this?"

"It's Wednesday."

"What month?"

"May."

"I'll be ninety-six years old next month. Lot of years to be on this earth. It's gone by like a blink."

"Time has a funny way of getting away from us," Leeann said. She scanned the half-acre of grass and trees. She wanted to ask about the note, why he'd written it, but there was plenty of time to get to that, plenty of time to tell him that lives changed as a result of what he'd done. But all Leeann could muster at that moment was, "Are they treating you well here?"

"Oh yes, we're treated well. But it's the ocean view that keeps me in this place."

Leeann nodded. She resisted the urge to dig up a handful of dandelions, roots and all, scattered on the grass nearby.

Dr. Turtle began speaking again but after a few words tumbled out, he stopped. He tried again and stopped. His eyes searched the sky as if confusion was setting in. He pulled a handkerchief from his pocket and wiped his mouth again.

"Dr. Turtle, something's bothering you."

Dr. Turtle took a breath and exhaled. "Leeann, your mother told me years ago that she feared your father had committed the arson in Berkshire Ridge. In fact, she said she was quite certain even though she had no proof. When a patient's relative tells me something in confidence, as she did, I should take those words to my grave." He used his handkerchief to wipe his mouth again. "But for some inexplicable reason, a few months ago, I told my son, a psychiatrist, what Helene Bright had told me." He looked away and swallowed hard. "My son urged me, in my own way, to tell the police or someone, whether it be publicly or anonymously. He thought I'd kept the confidence long enough. And he thought, if I told now, some good might come of it." Dr. Turtle strained his neck as if to get a better look at Leeann. "So this leads me to my question, Leeann. And it has kept me awake more than a few nights." He put his hands together, fingertips to fingertips.

Leeann leaned forward to make sure she heard Dr. Turtle's question. She had to steady herself in her chair, which wobbled in the wet earth.

"Do you think it has? Do you think some good has come out of what I did?"

"Dr. Turtle, no more sleepless nights." Leeann sliced her hand through the air, like an umpire calling a batter 'safe.' "It has. A *lot* of good. Good for the town, for the residents, for the police and fire. Traci's cleared her father's name. Good for me, now that the secret is no longer my burden."

Dr. Turtle's eyes brightened.

Leeann folded her hands in her lap. "Yes, without a doubt, my mother would have approved."

Leeann had been trying for days to reach Traci, leaving messages on her answering machine, rambling statements of apology and briefer messages saying she didn't blame her for ending their friendship. She received no reply. She called one more time on Friday morning, as she left the house to attend the nursery auction, and left another message.

The sun's brilliance dissolved into a chalky sky that pursued Leeann from Concord to the nursery in Haverhill. Ornamental grasses swayed at the nursery's entrance. A Butterfly bush was in full bloom, creating a purple wash against the white clapboard façade of the garden center. Beside it was Carolina allspice in deep red. She parked on the grassy shoulder in front of one of the greenhouses and walked to the white colonial where Ben was to meet her. After forty-five minutes she made her way to a stonewall and sat down. Where was he? He'd promised to meet her at nine. A gathering was forming in front of the auctioneer's table. Damn it, she told herself, walk across that street and buy that nursery. It's your time now. No more conflict, no more secret. Let go of the remorse for wasting so many years. She joined the gathering formed in front of the auctioneer's table.

Former nursery owner Dick Perios stepped from the greenhouse and sauntered Leeann's way. He held a can of soda and wore a Red Sox baseball cap, which he removed and put on Leeann's head.

"Don't need this anymore. I'm moving to New York."

Leeann kept her eye on the parking lot, still looking for Ben. She barely heard Dick ask if she had registered to bid.

"I'm about to."

In fact, Leeann was the only registered bidder among the handful of people standing in front of the auctioneer. Her ten-thousand-dollar cashier's check made her a legitimate participant. The auction began before she knew what was happening. The auctioneer announced the terms and conditions of the sale, stating the property would be sold "as is." In response to the opening bid, Leeann held up her paddle and three minutes later, the nursery was hers. She signed a purchase and sale agreement and was told she could close on the property in thirty days. The crowd dissipated, leaving Leeann with Dick, who congratulated her and assured her that she would do a better job of running the nursery than he did. Leeann looked over her newly purchased acres—the land, the main garden center, the house, the two greenhouses and the rich life growing inside and out. Her nursery, The Blue Iris, would thrive. She couldn't stand around any longer when there were so many to-do lists to write. Ben never arrived. She would wait for his call to explain why. Leeann knew what he would say.

Back home at noon, Leeann wanted to call a real estate broker and put her house on the market. Instead, she called Traci and was astonished when she picked up.

"You still talking to me?"

"What do you think?"

"Traci, I'm sorry, I'm a million times sorry."

"I just needed time to absorb all the news. I couldn't call you back right away."

The hesitation in Leeann's voice was thick. "You still willing…to see me?"

"Yeah, and I have you to thank for all the TV news trucks parked in front of my house wanting to interview me. They're looking for you too."

"I know. The media's been leaving me messages for days. I'm too busy to talk."

"Busy with what?"

"I bought the Silver Sword Nursery today, and I'm selling my house."

"I leave you alone for one week and you go and re-invent your life?"

"Listen, I want you at my house at four o'clock today. Bring your truck."

"Am I helping you move?"

"No, just be here with your truck."

A little after four, Leeann handed Traci a shovel and asked her to help dig up the eight rose bushes in the front yard.

"These going to your new house?" Traci asked.

"I just bought a nursery, I told you. I'll have more rose bushes than I know what to do with. These are going into your yard and you are going to learn to grow roses. Jimmy will help you. You can look at them day and night," Leeann said, slipping her shovel into the ground. "You should feel proud. You're a hero in Berkshire Ridge."

She took a break from digging and noticed Traci digging a little deeper and a little more rapidly than when she began. Traci rocked the ball of roots from side to side, as Leeann had shown her, and she didn't flinch when she grabbed a branch the wrong way and pierced her thumb with a thorn, leaving a bloody nick.

Leeann knew they would have plenty of daylight to finish the job. She knew they would have time to dig eight new holes in Traci's yard. They would kneel on the ground, lower each bush into a hole and spread out the roots. They would fertilize and fill up each hole. Leeann would sift her hands through the cool garden soil, which would have settled into her fingernails and nostrils by then, and would tell Traci not to call it dirt because soil was practically life itself and deserved to be called by its proper name. She would drape her hand over all the bushes before she left, feeling a paper-thin layer of evening dew on the leaves and flowers. And she would remember all eight bushes—the Bahia Roses with their red ruffled petals, the Medallion Roses with large apricot-tinted clusters, sometimes looking like the color of sunset, the Seashell Roses in salmon and coral colors. She cherished most her Lemon Spice hybrid tea, which had been wounded recently by an infestation of spotted cucumber beetles. Still damaged, it had mostly recovered. Almost every petal was unblemished now, except for one, a lone yellow, which was beautiful in its imperfection, its edges torn or sliced, with a little chip having been taken out of it by the infestation, leaving one jagged margin, inconspicuous in the circle of repeating, heart-shaped petals.

Epilogue: May, 2001

Clusters of pale purple lilacs draped the entrance of the Blue Iris Nursery. Throughout the day, Leeann handed out free bunches of Blue Iris to customers. She was celebrating the third anniversary of the purchase of her nursery. For the past three years, she has spent her days with her hands churning rich dark soil and surrounded by blooming flowers and lush greens. By afternoon, it occurred to her that she and Traci had traveled to California to confront Richard Bright three years earlier on that very day.

Shortly after Leeann purchased her new business, Jimmy was made vice president of his company, and he and Traci moved to North Carolina. Dr. Douglas Turtle died one month after Leeann's visit to Gloucester. She has stayed in touch with Ben, who quit his job in law to operate a full time DJ business throughout New England. Leeann never heard from her father.

Each Christmas since she moved south, Traci has sent Leeann a Christmas card and photo of her two growing daughters, Jessica and Amanda, born a year apart, posing with a smiling Santa. Every winter Leeann has remembered Traci with a bouquet of red roses on her birthday, New Year's Day.